ROMANTIC COMEDY

It was a dating wasteland out there.

Temple Burney had dated them all:

- Mr. Wandering Hands
- Mr. Put the Salt Shaker in your Purse
- Mr. Aren't I Wonderful

What Temple wanted:

- A man who was reliable, successful and fun to be with
- Gorgeous and sexy didn't hurt
- Wasn't that her best friend Craig?

Who said she couldn't fall in love with her best friend? It seemed to be working for "Friends'" Ross and Rachel. But Temple wasn't so sure. So far her love life was more like a horror flick than a popular sitcom.

Dear Reader,

Love and laughter—what a perfect marriage! And Harlequin owes you the readers thanks for our new, fun-filled, unfailingly romantic series. When we asked you what new stories you most wanted to read about, the answer came back loud and clear—romantic comedies!

What better way to end one of *those* days—the car wouldn't start, the boss wanted a huge report finished *yesterday,* the heel on your best pair of shoes broke on the way home—than with a good romantic comedy?

From classic movie couples like Hepburn and Tracy to the contemporary pairings of Meg Ryan and Tom Hanks, or Sandra Bullock and whomever (who doesn't look good next to Sandra?), we have always adored romantic comedies and the heroes and heroines in them.

So here it is. The lighter side of love. The first two Love & Laughter books. In *I Do, I Do...For Now* fabulous JoAnn Ross gives us a nineties twist on the marriage of convenience (Mitch is a guy who just can't say no). In *Dates and Other Nuts* Lori Copeland, well renowned for her humorous love stories, tackles the subject of dates from hell (sound a little *too* familiar?).

Settle back and enjoy. And remember, after you've smiled your way through these stories, there'll be more! Two brand-new books every month. Don't miss the love and laughter Kasey Michaels and Jennifer Crusie have in store for us in September. (Sneak preview: Fred, part basset, part beagle, part manic-depressive will play a starring role.) So please settle back and enjoy the beginning of a wonderful pairing—romantic comedies and you!

Humorously yours,

Malle Vallik
Associate Senior Editor

DATES AND OTHER NUTS
Lori Copeland

𝓗𝓪𝓻𝓵𝓮𝓺𝓾𝓲𝓷 𝓑𝓸𝓸𝓴𝓼

TORONTO • NEW YORK • LONDON
AMSTERDAM • PARIS • SYDNEY • HAMBURG
STOCKHOLM • ATHENS • TOKYO • MILAN
MADRID • WARSAW • BUDAPEST • AUCKLAND

ISBN 0-373-44002-2

DATES AND OTHER NUTS

Bestselling author **Lori Copeland,** a native of Springfield, Missouri, has had over forty novels published in the past thirteen years. Her humor and quick wit have made her books the recipient of numerous awards, including *Romantic Times* Reviewer's Choice and Career Achievement awards, as well as the *Affaire de Coeur* Gold and Silver Certificate awards.

Lori enjoys writing. No matter who the characters, or what the situation, she can't help but look at the funny side. When asked why she believes Love & Laughter is a natural pairing, she said, "There's a rare ailment that's about to break out across the land: giggleitis. It's a condition known to a rare breed of romance readers with a sensitive funny bone. A word of warning: consult your doctor before reading the Love & Laughter line. Giggleitis is highly contagious. The only antidote proven effective is the consumption of six ounces of chocolate between each chapter." Enjoy!

To Malle Vallik
for all her encouragement and support

1

"I DIDN'T TAKE the job, Grams." Having said the words, Temple Burney felt a burst of pride, savoring the elation of knowing she had made the right decision. Knew without a doubt!

At first when the home office had offered her an international-flight route, she'd been excited by the prospect of long-distance flights and more money. But her excitement had waned after she'd given the offer more thought. Admittedly, working for Sparrow Airlines as a commuter flight attendant lacked glamour, but she'd realized that more travel wasn't what she wanted at all.

In fact, she wanted less. She'd felt restless lately, unsettled. At times she wondered if it wasn't the loud ticking of her biological clock bugging her. There was that strange gnawing in the pit of her stomach when she saw couples walking hand in hand, looking content, obviously in love. She was determined to get the same thing for herself before it was too late.

As far as the money went, she had enough to get by. She was a good manager, and her nest egg was growing. Her assessing gaze swept over the small living room of the efficiency apartment she rented in Dallas. Her quarters were economical and cozy. Certainly adequate accommodation at this juncture of her life. Over the years, she'd even developed a deep affection for the owner of the building, Roberta King.

Roberta reminded her of Grams. The grandmotherly figure spoiled her almost as much as Grams did with all her home-baked pies, evening chats and fresh-cut roses from her garden. The woman's kitchen always smelled like home.

Temple knew that all of that was part of what was missing from her own life. It had hit her like a bolt of lightning on the way home from the interview yesterday. Suddenly she knew exactly what she wanted. Thirty-one, and she'd finally figured it out. She wanted to stay in Dallas, where she'd lived for the past five years, find Mr. Right and settle down. Career be hanged. Maybe it was no longer fashionable, but she wanted a husband, home and family.

"Didn't take the job!" Grams exclaimed. "Why not? I thought you were excited about the promotion."

Temple gripped the receiver. "I was—at first, but once I thought it over I decided against it. I like working for Sparrow and flying the commuters. It gives me time for a life. If I were flying international flights, I'd be gone all the time."

Her life was full, she reflected. She traveled whenever and wherever she wanted. Last summer, she and two other flight attendants, Thia Lambert and Sue Lisbon, had spent three weeks exploring Ireland. This spring, the three had visited Paris, then Brussels and Madrid. Switzerland was next. Then Australia the following year. New York during the Christmas season, New Orleans for Mardi Gras and Washington, D.C., during cherry-blossom time.

Between work, fitness workouts, monthly meetings with a group of colleagues who had formed an investment club, her volunteer work at a nearby nursing home and an active social life, she was always busy. The last thing she needed was added job pressure.

"Well, Tootie, I suppose you're old enough to know your own mind," Grams conceded. "My, you're like your mother in so many ways."

"Thanks, Grams," she said warmly. "That's a compliment."

"Yes, you're exactly like my Mary. Young, pretty, so solid for her age. She would have been very proud of you."

When Mary Burney died of a brain aneurysm a few years back, Grams had stepped in to fill the void. Temple smiled as she recalled hearing about how her grandmother had always been there to pick up the pieces. Including the dark days when Mary's young husband, Temple's father, was reported MIA in Vietnam. A navy pilot, Jack Burney had been shot down during the Tet offensive. Mary was alone and scared, with a new baby on the way. Eleanor Liddy had stepped in and made a home for Mary and Temple. A good, solid home.

Jack was still listed as MIA, but Temple had given up hoping that her father would ever come home. For years she had searched the newspapers for word of MIAs, and written her congressman. She'd even sent a letter to President Reagan, pleading for any information on her father the State Department could supply. The replies were compassionate, but led nowhere.

As with all MIA families, there was no body, no physical remains to grieve. The loss, the inability to achieve closure, had eaten away at her mother. Grams had filled any gaps in Temple's life with unconditional love.

Several years ago Temple realized she felt closest to her father's spirit when she was in a plane. Maybe because he loved them so. Twenty thousand feet aboveground, there were times she looked out the window and could see her father's face, a face she knew only from the picture she kept on her bedside table.

Like father, like daughter. She kinda liked that thought.

"So, that's my news, Grams," she said. "How are things in Summersville?"

"Oh, things in Summersville never change," Eleanor said with a chuckle. Temple knew the small town, located a hundred and fifty miles north of Dallas, was seldom disturbed by anything momentous. For her, that was part of its charm. "When are you coming to see me?" her grandmother asked.

"Soon, I hope. I'll have a few days off at the end of the month. Gee, I can hardly wait to tell Craig about my decision."

Eleanor smiled. "Helen and Frank Stevens's boy?"

"Yes."

"How is Craig?"

"Fine."

Actually, Craig was more than fine. He was FINE. Craig Stevens was her best friend. Grams wouldn't understand the special bond she and Craig shared—she'd make something romantic of it when it wasn't like that at all. In fact, Temple had a hard time defining the relationship herself. They had known each other nearly all their lives. They had grown up in the same small town, had gone to high school together. She'd lost track of him for a brief while. He'd gone away to the navy then gone to flight school; she'd gone on to college.

Five years ago she'd taken a job with Sparrow Airlines, whose main hub was in Dallas, and they'd bumped into each other again. An older, more experienced Craig, but nevertheless, Craig, her soul mate. He was a pilot for Sparrow, flying commuters because he preferred the more personal feel of the smaller plane and wanted less away-from-home time. Temple was surprised when he'd said he was still single. She wondered how, since he was about the best-looking guy she'd ever seen. In her opinion, Craig's dark, all-American looks made other men look like Quasimodo. When she'd blurted out that thought once, he'd laughed, saying he didn't have any trouble keeping women from lining up at his doorstep.

Temple found that hard to believe.

Their friendship had picked up where it had left off—as friends and confidants. Over the years they'd both seen their share of bad relationships, and they'd been there for each other.

Craig had nursed her through a bad time when she thought she'd found Mr. Right and the creep had turned out to be Mr. Rat instead. She'd cried inconsolably for days. Craig had stayed with her, wrapping her in her favorite afghan, combing her hair, making her chicken soup, holding her on his lap by the fire as she cried and asked why, why her? Why couldn't she find the man of her dreams?

When his turn came, she'd been by his side. He'd had a brief relationship with one of her close friends, Nancy Johnson. For a while it had looked like wedding bells were imminent for the two, but the next thing Temple knew they'd split up.

Craig refused to say what had happened. And the only thing Nancy would say was that she was heartbroken about the split, and hoped they could mend the rift someday.

During the trying ordeal, Temple had treated Craig like the lost puppy she'd cared for one summer. She'd baked his favorite cookies, and sat through hours of "The Three Stooges," until she thought she'd lose her mind. Only for Craig would she have endured Curly, Larry and Moe.

Craig and Nancy hadn't reconciled, but Temple and Nancy had kept in touch and it was clear the torch was still burning.

Why she and Craig had failed to click romantically, Temple couldn't say. It certainly wasn't Craig's lack of appeal quotient. He was about the best pilot in the cockpit, as well as in the looks department. If she'd ever thought she was less than objective about that, all she had to do was watch female heads turn as he strode through the terminal.

Craig was an important element in her life. Without him, she'd never balance a checkbook, have a properly filed tax return or that much-needed broad shoulder to cry on. They were good, trusting friends. Not many people enjoyed that kind of blessing.

"Are you and Craig dating?" Eleanor asked.

"No, Grams. We're just friends."

Here it comes, Temple thought, mouthing the words simultaneously with Grams.

"Well, are you dating anyone?"

"Uh-huh, a few, now and then." Actually, she'd been dating her brains out trying to find the perfect mate. Books on the subject all said the perfect man was out there, but so far she hadn't run into him. Just a lot of losers she wouldn't spend an afternoon with, let alone a lifetime.

"Oh? Anyone interesting?"

"Nope. I'm shooting for the biggest bores I can find."

Though what she'd said was meant to be a joke, Temple winced when she realized how close she'd come to the truth. She didn't intentionally pick out jerks. They just seemed to be attracted to her, as if there were a sign on her forehead that said, Bore Me, Irritate Me, I Love a Wasted Evening.

"I'm looking forward to seeing you settled down, Tootie, and starting your own family," Eleanor gently urged her.

"I know, Grams." How could she not know? Grams was eager to see her grandchildren, or great-grandchildren, that is, and reminded Temple every chance she got.

Glancing at her watch, Temple realized she had only a few minutes before her date picked her up. "Oh, by the way, I got my hair cut."

"Oh, Temple!" Impatience tinged Gram's voice. "Why ever would you cut that glorious mane of auburn hair?"

"I was tired of the hassle, Grams," she explained patiently. "It took hours to dry."

"I know, but it was so beautiful—why, you haven't cut it since you were a little girl. You'll ruin your looks."

"My looks, such as they are, are intact, Grams. It's not that short, just a nice sporty wedge."

"A wedge! Oh dear. Like that ice skater's?"

"Dorothy Hammill was fifteen years ago. It's a little more modern, Grams."

"Oh, my."

"It looks good, Grams. Make's me look older, more sophisticated."

"I hope not too old."

Just then, the doorbell rang.

"Got to go, Grams."

"Oh? Do you have a date?"

"Yes, I have a date." Friday night and she had a date. The first step in her serious finding-a-man game plan. She was adamant about this, although she wasn't telling Grams until she had Mr. Fabulous in the chute with the gate shut.

"With whom?"

"Darrell somebody."

"Does he come from a nice family?"

"I'll ask, Grams. Talk to you Sunday."

She hung up, and hurriedly checked her appearance in the hall mirror. Fussing with her hair, she groaned. Why did she get it cut! She looked peeled. Geez, what would Darrell— Darrell—what was his last name? She couldn't remember. They'd met only briefly at a party last week.

Darrell, er—something—er—other. This was agony! *Why do I put myself through this? I have a bad feeling about this, a very bad feeling. It's going to be another date from hell, I can feel it.*

Leaning closer to the mirror, she checked her lipstick. Wrong color. It made her look washed-out and sick.

The doorbell rang again. Too late.

Turning, she inspected her ensemble. *I should have worn something else—I look fat. Maybe it's not too late to change.*

Darrell, Darrell? Shoot! What was his last name? She drew a complete blank. She'd have to fake her way through the situation until she could figure it out.

He works for a law firm—no, a construction company.

Pivoting, she studied her reflection, and grimaced. The blue outfit would have been more comfortable. This was cooler, but the blue fit her better. No, if she was going to sweat, she was going to be comfortable.

We're going to Mammal World this afternoon. That I know.

Temple winced at the thought. Dallas, August, Mammal World. Hot, hot, hot. Dinner in an air-conditioned restaurant would have been her preference. Maybe hers and Craig's favorite haunt, the Bird's Nest, where the prime rib melts in your mouth? Definitely preferable.

Past experience prompted her to drop a bottle of aspirin in her purse. She gave her appearance a final once-over as the doorbell rang a third time. Taking a deep breath, she prepared to meet her fate.

Good luck, she thought.

Instinct told her she was going to need it.

2

"YOU AND STEPHANIE have plans for the weekend?" Craig asked.

"We're putting in new shrubs."

Jim Scott, known affectionately as Scotty, had dropped by to return a movie. He channel-surfed while he waited for Craig to finish dressing.

Over the years the two men had flown together often, Jim as first officer for Sparrow Airlines and Craig as pilot. They'd developed a close friendship.

Scotty was married. So happily married he thought everyone else should be. Consequently, he was a pain about the subject to his single friends, especially Craig Stevens.

"Who did you say you were going out with tonight?" he asked.

"Nina Jennings."

"Cute." Scotty paused the remote on HBO and watched for a moment. "Dinner?"

Craig nodded.

Glancing at his watch, Scotty frowned. "Saturday night starts early with you. It's only three."

"I have a few errands to run before I pick up Nina."

"You don't sound very excited about the prospect."

Frowning, Craig redid his tie. "Frankly, I wish I hadn't made the date."

"You're getting too set in your ways. Look at you, you've got your 'dating' clothes on."

"What's wrong with my clothes?" Craig briefly assessed his image in the mirror. Blue blazer, khaki pants, blue oxford shirt, red-striped tie.

"You dress as if you're on your way to an execution instead of a night on the town."

"I feel like I'm going to an execution. My own."

Thirty-two, single and not the least worried about it, he would have preferred to stay home and enjoy a glass of good wine while listening to classical CDs.

Unfortunately, his well-meaning friends didn't believe that he was happy with his marital status. They kept setting him up with matrimonial prospects. For some reason—probably some psychological flaw—he kept agreeing to go. It wasn't that he was anti-marriage, just not in any rush to advance the idea. He believed in doing a lot of looking before buying anything, especially a wedding ring. He was the sort of man who kicked the tires, honked the horn and checked the mileage before driving off the lot. He didn't like surprises.

Tonight's goddess du jour was Nina, a computer programmer for the airline. He had met her once, briefly. Before he'd known it, a mutual friend had insisted he ask her out. So here he was, getting ready for a date he didn't want to go on. He was afraid his life was becoming too much like a popular Thursday-evening sitcom.

"Ever been serious about a woman?" Scotty asked.

"Once."

"Yeah? So what happened?"

"Didn't work out." Craig stared back at his reflection in the mirror, trying to keep a straight face. Saying that Nancy didn't "work out" was like referring to Hurricane Andrew as a spring shower. Not many people knew about that unfortunate episode in his life.

"Who was she?"

"A girl I met when I first started with Sparrow."

"What was she like?"

"Like?"

"Well, I mean, this is the only girl I've ever heard you admit you might have been serious about. What was she like?"

"Blond, blue-eyed, great laugh, flight attendant. We had everything in common. I was beginning to think she was the one."

"And?"

"She wasn't. I woke up and realized I couldn't picture myself sitting across the breakfast table from her every morning. So, I got out of bed and phoned her. Asked her to meet me for breakfast." He smiled wryly at the memory. "The fact that it was five in the morning didn't help."

Scotty whistled under his breath. "Did she go ballistic when you broke it off?"

"Full thrust."

"Bummer."

"Two days later, she persuaded the super to let her into my apartment. When I got home, I found she'd squashed Preparation H into every piece of furniture I owned."

"Preparation H?"

"She said it was appropriate, considering."

Scotty winced. "Ouch."

"The following week, she broke into my car and ground bananas into the dashboard. It was summer, ninety-five degrees outside, a hundred and ten in the car."

"Ex from hell." Scotty shook his head in sympathy.

"Yeah. For the next month the interior of that Ford looked like a Christmas tree, with all those pine-scented air fresheners hanging in it. I finally had to sell it."

"That was the end of it?"

"No, I had to move and have my phone unlisted. Still, for the next five years, she'd find me and call to remind me what a heel I was."

"Bitter, huh?"

"Bitter?" Craig laughed hollowly. "I guess you could say that."

"Heard from her lately?"

"No, actually, I don't know what happened to her, don't want to know."

"Well, you can't let one bad experience sour you on women."

Picking up his jacket, Craig smiled. "But then, I don't plan to get into that kind of situation again, either." He liked his life. He wished his friends could believe that. Why couldn't they understand he liked quiet amusement? Fishing, hiking, going to the library. They were too anxious to get him mated for life. He wanted that. Someday. Just not now.

"Ever think about Temple?"

"Think what about Temple?"

Craig straightened his tie unnecessarily. Think about her? It was hard not to. Temple Burney was gorgeous, had a great sense of humor, had great legs, was a great flight attendant and had great legs. Unfortunately, he hadn't managed to get her to think of him as anything other than a friend. Quite often he had more than friendly feelings toward Temple, but he didn't want to ruin what they had. Could Temple be his Mrs. Right? Shrugging, he shook his head. He'd never convince her.

"About dating her."

Craig stuffed keys and billfold into his pockets. "We're just friends."

"Too bad. You two make a great couple."

"Temple doesn't date pilots."

"Yeah. What's that all about? Was she burned by one at some time?"

"Not exactly. She's just paranoid about pilots and marriage. She wants to keep work and pleasure separate."

"I don't get it."

"Her father was a pilot in Nam," he explained. "His plane was shot down during the Tet offensive in '68. He's been MIA for the past twenty-seven years. Her mother didn't handle it well and it's made Temple pilot-shy."

"Too bad."

Craig shrugged into his jacket. "Well, she may not date pilots, but that doesn't mean she ignores them. She's got a bad case of one-upmanship going with me."

"The infamous race for the parking space each morning?" Scott couldn't contain his smile.

Craig smiled back. "She's good at lane sharking."

Laughing, Scotty snagged his jacket and followed Craig to the door.

"Hey, why don't you stop by tomorrow night?" Scotty said. "Steph would love to see you. I'll ask her to fix those stuffed pork chops you like."

For a moment, Craig fantasized about coming home to someone every night who cooked his favorite food, shared his day, slept next to him every night.

"You're on," Craig said, flipping out the lights and locking the door.

As they started down the stairway of the two-story apartment building, Craig reconsidered his friend's invitation.

"You wouldn't be planning to fix me up with another date, would you?"

Scotty looked wounded. "Would I do that to a friend?"

"Ha! I come for pork chops and get cheesecake every time."

Scotty dismissed the accusation with a cheerful wave. "See you at seven tomorrow night."

ACROSS TOWN, Temple opened the door, trying to look friendly.

"Darrell?" Her eyes traveled his length. *Who the hell is this? Did I make a date with this guy?* She'd only had one drink that night. Surely she hadn't been that bombed.

"THAT'S ME, BABE!"

His megaphone voice blasted her back a step.

Darrell, dressed in plaid seat-cover trousers, a hot-pink polo shirt and white patent-leather shoes, grinned back at her. His panama hat with a Hawaiian headband had a plastic pineapple stuck in it. A neon fanny pouch was strapped around his middle.

"YOU'RE TEMPLE!"

At the moment, she wished she was anyone but Temple. Taking another step backward, she managed a weak, "How nice to see you again. Would you like to come in?"

"THANKS, BUT I LEFT THE CAR RUNNING. YOU ABOUT READY?"

Temple reached for her purse, wondering if he had a hearing problem. Her eyes searched for a telltale wire to indicate he had Walkman headphones or a hearing aid in his ear, but there wasn't any.

"HOPE YOU LIKE DOLPHINS!"

"Love them," she murmured.

"TURNED OUT TO BE A NICE DAY, DIDN'T IT?" Darrell boomed as they walked outside to his car.

Temple waved at Mrs. King watering her flowers.

"THAT LITTLE SHOWER WE HAD EARLIER SCARED ME. THOUGHT IT MIGHT RAIN US OUT!"

Mrs. King dropped her watering can and looked around, startled.

Nodding, Temple cringed. She thought back to when they'd been introduced at the party and remembered that the room had been exceptionally crowded, so much so they had had to shout above the din. At least she'd thought he was shouting.

"HOPE YOU LIKE DOLPHINS!" he repeated as he helped her settle in the passenger side of the car, then walked around to the driver's side and got in.

Looking over, he grinned. "READY?"

Smiling lamely, she nodded. "Ready."

She noticed that two other neighbors had stopped working in their yards and were looking in their direction.

During the drive, Temple tried to concentrate on the conversation but she kept wincing. Every time Darrell opened his mouth to speak he jacked up the volume.

"YOU DON'T TALK MUCH, DO YOU? WELL, THAT'S ALL RIGHT. I LIKE QUIET WOMEN." He laughed. "HAR snort HAR snort."

Temple rolled her eyes. It's happening again.

As the two large, green, concrete dolphins marking the entrance to Mammal World came into view, she had started to think of Darrell as one large, living, breathing megaphone.

One, unfortunately, she was stuck with all afternoon.

"HEY!"

A young couple walking ahead of them whirled to answer. When they saw he was speaking to Temple, not to the park attendant five hundred yards away, they turned back.

"Yes?"

"HERE WE ARE!"

Yes. Here I am.

Mammal World was bustling. Temple and Darrell made their way toward an open-air stadium.

"WANT SOMETHING TO DRINK? IT'S AWFUL HOT!"

Hot? She'd wager hell was cooler than the asphalt parking lot at Mammal World.

"Thanks, a cola would be nice."

"I'LL GET US ONE!" With that, he walked toward the refreshments stand.

He returned a few minutes later with drinks and snacks. As they elbowed their way into the Dolphin Stadium, she tried to balance the large cola and tub of popcorn Darrell had bought. Someone stepped on her heel and she swallowed a yelp. If pain was an indicator, she was crippled for life.

"YOU HURT?"

Five people turned to see if he was speaking to them.

"No, I'm fine, really."

"YOU SURE? WANT TO SIT DOWN FOR A MINUTE?"

Six more heads swiveled, looking for the loud voice.

Apologies were hurriedly exchanged. Temple walked on tiptoe with her shoe heel flopping as the mob shoved her through the gates.

Her gaze went immediately to the top rows of seats, out of the blistering sun, but Darrell quickly dashed her hopes.

"I LIKE TO SIT UP CLOSE, IF YOU DON'T MIND."

He made a beeline for the front row, motioning for Temple to follow.

Snapping open the stadium seat he carried with him, Darrell carefully positioned it on the bleacher and made himself comfortable. Setting aside the popcorn and drink, Temple fished in her purse for a clean tissue and wiped the wet, backless hot-as-hell bench and sat down. Again, she thought back to the party where they'd met. Darrell had seemed so much less . . . well . . . irritating.

Munching popcorn, she listened to a young, tanned girl in skimpy shorts and a halter top make the opening announcements.

"Hi, my name is Julie!"

Applause.

Okay, Temple decided. This could be okay.

Settling herself on the hot bleacher, she reassured herself this wasn't so bad. Maybe it would even be fun.

"This afternoon, Rocco and Tuffy, our bottlenose dolphins, are going to perform for you."

Applause. Applause.

Julie's voice faded as Temple focused on the two, large dolphins lazily circling the edge of the pool. The sun sparkled on the water and beat down on her head. The steel bleachers were like solar units turning the stadium bowl into a giant wok.

Sipping cola through a straw, wishing she'd brought a hat, Temple dug into the popcorn again.

"ISN'T THIS GREAT!" Darrell blared, leaning closer. "YOU'RE GOING TO GET A KICK OUT OF THIS!"

She forced a smile, seriously doubting she was going to like anything about it, despite her earlier reassurances. By now, she was pretty sure the only kick she was likely to get was a self-executed one.

"And coming out of the water," Julie said in a voice brimming with enthusiasm, "Rocco will leap twelve feet into the air, perform a triple somersault, before diving back into the pool!"

Julie was too perky. Temple didn't like perky.

Applause, and more applause, accompanied by a few loud stomps and whistles.

The two dolphins darted swiftly around the pool. Sliding out of the water onto a ramp, they inhaled the fish Julie dropped into their open mouths.

Chattering noisily, Rocco and Tuffy took several cheesy bows while the crowd clapped.

Temple took another sip of cola.

It's as hot as blue blazes in here. Grams, I hope you appreciate this.

Slipping back into the water, the dolphins swam around, picking up speed. In no time, Rocco was doing seventy around the pool's perimeter.

Fascinated in spite of herself by the animals' artistry, Temple edged forward in her seat to get a better look as she absently nibbled popcorn.

Suddenly, Rocco torpedoed out of the water, made a sharp ten-foot arc in the air and flipped three times before plunging back into the crystal-blue water.

Temple heard the sharp crack of four hundred pounds of mammal flesh splitting water at precisely the same time a twenty-foot wall of water swamped her.

The impact bowled her backward, knocking the cola out of her hand and sending her popcorn flying.

Stunned, she lay in a pool of fishy-smelling water, staring sightlessly at the sky, while everyone clapped at Rocco's fine performance.

"COOL!" Darrell shouted, apparently not bothered by the tidal wave. There wasn't a dry thread on him, nor on anyone else seated in rows one through six.

Realizing her feet were sticking straight up in the air, giving Darrell and the fifteen hundred others around him a bird's-eye view of her Victoria's Secrets, Temple rolled over and sat up. She knew her mascara lay in black puddles underneath her eyes, and she could feel her hair slicked to her head in irregular waves.

Darrell glanced over. "NEED A HAND?"

Humiliated, the old gag line *Need a hand?* and someone clapped, popped into Temple's mind.

Before she could stop him, he'd jerked her upright.

Landing on her feet, she frantically strained soggy popcorn through her teeth to keep from choking. The pungent fish odor radiating from her blouse was nauseating. She stood for a moment, trying to get her bearings. She was afraid to lick her lips. She was fairly certain that dolphin water wasn't sanitary.

Absently tapping her on the back, Darrell's gaze remained fixed on the show.

"WATER FELT GOOD, DIDN'T IT!"

By now, Temple could feel every eye in the stadium centered on them, and the spectacle she'd just made of herself.

"Great!"

Her hair hung in matted, wet clumps around her face, streaming with water. She plucked at her blouse, pulling it away from her skin in a futile effort to keep what Grams would call "decent."

When the show was over, Darrell suggested they go directly to the Shumay the Killer Whale show.

Hear that, Grams? Shumay. Killer whale. Happy?

Limping up the stairs to her front door later that afternoon, Temple turned to wave goodbye to Darrell with rabid relief that the day was finally over.

Inside her apartment, she collapsed on the sofa. Her clothes were sticking to her like clammy cheesecloth. Her hair would take a week of reconditioning. Her shoulders and nose were sunburned. Her feet felt as if she'd walked barefoot over a bed of hot coals, her sandals were ruined and the backs of her heels were turning purple.

Staring at the ceiling, Temple groaned. She knew finding Mr. Wonderful wasn't going to be easy, but this was ridiculous.

She wasn't operating under the Law of Averages; she was cursed by Murphy's Law.

3

FLO LARSON, who ran the car rental booth at Dallas/Fort Worth Airport, leaned back in her seat and lit a cigarette, clearly enjoying the twenty-minute ride to the airport.

"You threw him out a second-story window? It's a wonder you didn't kill the poor man," Temple marveled. Edgar Winters was eighty-three years old if he was a day!

"Aw, didn't hurt anything but the old goat's pride." Flo took another drag from her cigarette before biting into a glazed doughnut. Temple could practically hear the cholesterol, fat, and triglycerides explode in Flo's veins.

"Flo, why?"

"Like I said. I caught him in bed with Ruthie Fredericks."

"And you actually picked him up and threw him out the window?"

The lively seventy-year-old grinned guilelessly. "I figured if the old fart thought he could make love to a woman at his age, he probably thought he could fly, too."

Temple smiled, and kept on driving. Morning traffic around the airport was unusually light. She exited the highway and drove her pickup toward the employee parking area, her gaze fixed on the rearview mirror.

Flo finished her cigarette and doughnut about the same time. Hitting the automatic window button, she pitched the butt and stuffed the bakery tissue containing doughnut crumbs into her coat pocket. Flipping down the visor mirror, she examined her teeth for pastry residue, brushing at her chin and mouth.

"What time's your flight?" the older woman asked.

"Seven."

"St. Louis?"

"Uh-huh, and all points between."

Flo rummaged through her purse for a tube of lipstick. "Thanks for the ride. Guess I'll have to break down and buy a new battery. Makes twice this week the Pinto wouldn't start."

Still watching the rearview mirror intently, Temple only half listened to Flo.

"Who are you flying with this morning?"

"Stevens and Scott."

Temple glanced out the side-view window. Craig's white Lincoln should be turning off the highway any minute. Strange how much more she looked forward to a flight when she knew they would be working together.

Flo shook her head. "You and Craig are like a couple of kids," she declared. "Torment the life out of each other. You two play this parking-space game every morning?"

"Every morning we fly together."

"Funny you two never got together. You know, Craig's good-looking, successful," Flo remarked. "You're good-looking, successful— 'Everybody good-lookin' an' successful,'" she sang in an uplifting, spiritual rhythm with a snap of her fingers.

"Craig and me?" Temple laughed. "No sky jockeys for me."

Pilots were off her list. Even Craig. Not even for Mr. Right. For some reason, though, he'd been looking awful good to her lately.

"Besides, he was engaged to my best friend once," she told Flo. "Things didn't work out and she was deeply hurt. She's still carrying a torch for him. I just wouldn't do that to her."

"Temple, you're too nice for your own good."

"That's me. Took my Girl Scout oath to heart."

"Hmmph," Flo said, stripping the cap off her lipstick. She'd just touched the color to her lips when Temple spotted Craig's Lincoln and floored the pickup. The truck shot forward, pinning Flo's neck to the headrest, sending a bright slash of Moroccan Sunset lipstick streaking past her nose.

Stamping the accelerator to the floor, Temple grinned devilishly when she saw Craig's car spurt forward.

Flo struggled to right herself, clinging to the door handle as the two vehicles raced side by side along the outer road. Craig tried to shut Temple out at the turn, but failed.

Whipping into her parking spot, Temple slammed on the brakes and cut the engine. Her '87 GMC Silverado precisely straddled the line between the two spaces in top-notch line-straddling form. Weeks of practice were paying off. She rarely missed her mark these days.

The Lincoln pulled up and squalled to a halt. Backing up, Craig made several attempts to maneuver the automobile into the tight space Temple had left. The power steering screeched as he worked to manipulate the big car into the narrow opening. The grating sound of tire rubbing against concrete shattered the silence.

Reading Craig's lips, Temple laughed and waited as Flo, used to their antics, slid across to the driver's side to exit. He managed to wedge the door open, but had to maneuver sideways to squeeze out.

"Hi, Captain Stevens. Beautiful morning, isn't it?" she said cheerfully.

Craig reached inside the car for his jacket and flight bag and slammed the door. Inspecting the curbed tires—scuffs of powdery white ringed both the left front and rear—he shook his head in disgust.

"Lane shark."

"Poor loser."

Flo, still wiping lipstick off her nose, walked ahead of them to the terminal. Eyeing Temple's battered pickup, Craig fell into step with her.

"When are you going to get a decent car?"

"When that ole used car lot in th' sky comes to claim her." She drawled, grinning in the direction of her truck. "You look beat. Hard times?"

"The worst. How about you?"

"Terrible."

His crystal-blue gaze measured her with the practiced eye of a man who makes his living on quick estimates. "How was your date with . . . Darrell, wasn't it?"

"All noise—no spark. How was your week?"

"Let's see . . . Sunday night was the pits. Scott rickey-dooed me again. I went for dinner, and got stuck with his cousin from Little Rock."

"Oh? How about your date on Saturday night?"

"Nina wanted to go to a movie."

"Yeah? Have a good time?"

Craig's amusement faded. "Nina has a deviated septum."

"Really?"

"Have you ever sat next to someone in a movie theater with a deviated septum?"

"I don't think so."

"Her right nostril. She couldn't breathe. Everyone within three rows of us knew it."

"Sounds like fun."

"Oh, Nina was a breeze compared to Geneva. She was Jeff's choice for me for Monday night. You don't want to hear about her."

Temple laughed as they entered the airport lobby together. The commuter terminal was bustling this morning. Sparrow counters were country blue with the large maroon Sparrow Airlines logo prominently displayed on the back wall of each section.

Smiling hello to Ginny, who was wiping down her lunch counter, they parted—Craig to check in, Temple to grab a quick cup of coffee. Ginny had been on a week's vacation so they were seriously behind on gossip.

The vivacious redhead glanced up as Temple dropped her flight bag on the floor and slid onto a stool at the counter. "How'd it go Friday night?" It was Ginny's party where she'd met Darrell.

"Ginny, does Darrell have a hearing problem?"

Ginny frowned. "Oh. You mean about him talking too loud?"

Temple nodded. "Yeah, about that."

"I don't think so... I know his family. The whole bunch talk loud for some reason."

"Thanks for telling me."

"No go?"

"My ears rang all night!"

"Let's see—" Ginny checked an imaginary list "—that must be prospect number three this month?"

Temple studied her sunburned nose in the mirror hanging behind the counter. She still looked like Rudolph the Red-Nose Reindeer.

Ginny leaned on the counter, her brown eyes quizzical. "I thought Darrell might make the cut. So he talks a little loud. It could be worse."

Temple's eyes met her friend's. "Yeah? Like how much worse?"

Ginny's eyebrows lifted into a look of innocence. "He could be twins?"

Sighing, Temple reached for the sugar. "Maybe I should give up on finding Mr. Spectacular and just buy a cat."

"Persians are good," Ginny agreed sagely. "Independent. Feed them once a day, empty their box every other day or so. They purr nice, lick your hand once in a while. Shed very little if you keep them brushed. When you get tired of looking at them, you can lock them in the laundry room. They don't lose their shoes, keys or billfold and they don't snore."

Even if she locked Darrell in the laundry room, she'd still hear him.

The whole town would hear him.

Again, Temple studied her reflection in the mirror, wondering if she had time to do something about her nose as she watched the traffic of passengers in various states of haste passing behind her.

Couples were parting with hugs, kisses and tearful smiles. For a moment, she felt a pang of envy which she quickly pushed aside.

"I don't know how you do it, Gin. You and Mike have gone together for what? Two years?"

Temple couldn't find a man who held her interest for more than two days. Not even for Grams. Lately she could hardly make it through four hours with one.

"Are you two thinking of marriage?"

Ginny shrugged and poured ketchup into plastic bottles. "I don't know. There are still some things to work out," she said. "Mike's not crazy about children and I want a houseful."

"He'll come around."

"I'm not counting on it. He had my Chia Pet spayed for my birthday."

Grinning, Temple glanced at her watch, took a last sip of coffee and slid off the stool. "Running late. See you later."

"Hey," Ginny called. "Your birthday's coming up. Shall I start looking for a cat?"

"I'll think about it," Temple said, heading toward the exit. The idea was sounding better to her all the time.

Scotty was in the copilot seat, clipboard in hand, going down the preflight list when Temple stepped inside the door of the small cockpit.

"Coffee, gentlemen?"

"Love of my life," Scotty said, taking one cup.

This morning's flight was aboard a Saab 340 aircraft with a crew of three: pilot, first officer and flight attendant. The aircraft, with one-by-two seating, represented a whole new generation of planes built especially for shorter-distance flying. The cockpit was equipped with state-of-the-art avionics technology. It was one of Temple's favorite planes.

Squeezing around her, Craig took his seat at the controls. The rush of heat at the unexpected contact took Temple by surprise. It was all-encompassing, like being bathed in tropical sunlight. Her cheeks flamed and she stared at him, trying to understand what had happened.

Craig took the cup of coffee from her. "Something wrong?"

"No, uh... everything's fine, thanks." What was that about? Shivers for Craig Stevens? Since when? Just because he was wearing Old Spice after-shave, her absolute favorite.

Scotty sipped his coffee gratefully. "Didn't have time for any at home this morning. Steph was up all night with the baby."

"Nothing serious, I hope?" Temple leaned against the door frame, her equilibrium regained.

"Teething." Laying aside the clipboard, Scotty took another sip of his coffee. "Funny how quick you forget things," he said. "Pete and Cari are five and six now. Steph and I had forgotten the number of times we had to get up at night to massage sore gums and try to get aspirin down a baby. But, alas, I see I bore you." He grinned.

Craig settled his sunglasses on his nose and adjusted them. Temple noticed the way his hair lay smoothly against the nape of his neck, the attractive way the crisp, navy and light blue uniform fit him like a glove, defining his broad shoulders and muscled thighs—

Geez, Burney, what is the matter with you? Craig's your best friend? You're ogling him like a potential, clandestine lover! Ooohh, now there's a thought.

Shaking the fantasy aside, she made herself concentrate on what Scotty was saying.

"You two need to find somebody and settle down." He handed his cup back to Temple. "Stop all this running around with strangers, going home alone, waking up to Pop-Tarts in the toaster and instant coffee."

"You sound like Grams," she said.

"I like Pop-Tarts," Craig grunted, frowning at his clipboard.

"Eleven years tomorrow I asked Steph to marry me, and miracle of miracles she said yes. We're getting a sitter and going out to dinner Friday night."

"Wow," Temple teased, underwhelmed by the plans.

"Hey, don't knock it. It may not be laser lights and rockets, but it's nice. Comfortable. The kind of familiarity that makes it—" He stopped midsentence, looking a little embarrassed at his pleasure in the relationship he shared with his wife. "Well, we'll have a quiet, candlelight dinner with wine, then home—to bed. Early." He winked at Craig. "It's not bad. Trust me."

Smothering a sigh of frustration, Temple retrieved Craig's coffee cup. "I envy you, Scotty. Find me a man just like Steph, and I'll marry him on the spot."

"Just like Steph?"

"Well." She grinned. "With a few significant differences."

Stowing his clipboard, Craig began final preparations. "Can't you two think of anything but marriage?"

"Giving you the creepy-crawlies?" Scotty laughed.

"Not me," Temple said easily, aware Craig was as shy of matrimony as she had once been. "I wish I could find Mr. Marvelous."

"You're looking at him, sweetheart." Winking, Craig smiled at her and her pulse jumped erratically at the familiar gesture. It wasn't unusual for him to wink at her, but this morning it seemed somehow different.

"Maybe you're looking in the wrong places," Craig mused aloud, studying a chart.

"You'd think I was looking under rocks, judging by the candidates I've been coming up with," she said dryly. "Just tell me where to look, and I'll gladly check it out."

"If I knew, I'd be looking there myself." Putting away the chart, he smiled. "All okay. Ready to get these people to their destinations?"

Temple saluted, smiling. "Aye, aye, Captain."

Later, she did what she did best. She took care of her passengers, the part of her job she never tired of. Over the years, she'd formed numerous friendships with frequent fliers, keeping in touch by Christmas cards and an occasional letter.

"Nuts?

"Coffee, juice or soft drink?

"I'm sure you'll be at your gate on time.

"No, ma'am, it's perfectly safe to use the lavatory when the plane is banking.

"No, ma'am, really. You won't fall out.

"Magazine?

"Another aircraft? Yes, sir, I'm sure the captain is aware of its presence. Yes, I'll bring it to his attention—just in case.

"Just a noise, ma'am. No, I don't think anything's wrong with the engine. I can't identify the source, but it's nothing to be concerned about."

The usual questions, usual answers, but important to the passengers.

Ten hours and seven touchdowns later, they landed back in Dallas. With the last passenger disembarked, the galley secured, magazines returned to their places, Temple picked up her shoulder bag and stuck her head into the pilots' compartment.

"Need anything?"

"Nope, just about ready to go," Scotty said, reading off the last two items of the post-flight check.

Five minutes later, the three of them were striding toward the terminal.

"What's on for tonight, Scotty?" Craig asked.

"Quiet night at home."

"How about you, Burney? Got a hot date?"

There it was again. A ting . . . a delicious little wave when he spoke to her.

"Not even a lukewarm one."

"No date? Something wrong?"

"No, just tired."

"Too many late nights," he teased.

"Sure, just like yours."

"Anyone game for breakfast in the morning before our flight?" Craig asked.

"Not me," Scotty said. "On these hours, I can't eat before noon."

"Temple?"

"Not me. That would mean getting up an hour earlier. Can't do it."

Tempting, but keep your distance, Burney. Your libido is acting weird around him lately.

"Lazy?"

"Pathetically so."

Touching his fingertip to the bill of his hat, Craig strode down the concourse, leaving Temple and Scotty behind.

Temple felt a niggling of regret as she watched him go. She would have liked nothing better than to have breakfast with him, but until she figured out what was going on with her, she couldn't chance it. Making a fool of herself with Craig was the last thing she wanted to do.

"Hey," Scotty said. "Why don't you come over for dinner next week? Stephanie mentioned the other day that it's been a long time since you two have seen each other."

Temple hesitated, knowing Scotty's penchant for fixing her up.

"Hey, do me a favor. Let me screw up my own life. I'm good at it."

"Oh! I'm hurt." Scotty's shoulders slumped and there was a basset hound look on his face. "I thought you liked my friends."

"No, I like you and Steph as friends. I haven't yet met one of your fix-ups that I could stand."

"Honest, Steph wants you to come to dinner," he insisted. "How about it?"

"Are you sure Steph wants company for dinner in the middle of the week? How about I drop by for dessert?"

"No, she'll want you to come for dinner. How about it, kiddo?"

Why fight it, Temple? You're actively seeking Don Juan, remember? Work at this!

"All right," she said finally. "It has been a long time since I've seen Steph and the kids. Let me know what time and what I can bring."

"Will do."

Temple watched Scotty stride toward a bank of telephones to let his wife know he'd landed safely. Steph would be waiting for the call. And who was waiting for her call? Nobody. Would there ever be someone? Was she ready for that? Yes. With the right guy.

Her gaze drifted back over the concourse, hoping to catch a glimpse of Craig, but he was already gone. What was this empty feeling?

Shrugging mentally, she waved at Ginny and headed for the parking lot.

CRAIG HAD JUST WALKED into his apartment when the phone rang. Tired from the long day, he picked up the receiver, frowning when he heard Jeff Sharp's voice on the other end.

"Hi, Jeff, what's up?"

He listened, wincing inwardly.

"Boy, I'd like to help you out, but—

"Yeah, she sounds nice, but I—

"What about Sam?

"Can't Suzy set her up with one of her friends?

"No, I had a busy weekend. I think I'll stay home and heat a TV dinner, relax—

"Sure, it can keep, but—"

He drew a deep breath. First Scotty, and now Jeff. He was going to have to put his foot down.

"Well, if she's already bought the tickets. What time?

"Yes, it'd be a shame to let the tickets go to waste. Are you and Lynda going?

"Come on, Jeff. You want me to go, but you're not going?

"Okay, tell Gina I'll pick her up around—" he glanced at his watch "—seven-thirty."

Dropping the phone into its cradle, he shrugged out of his jacket.

Damn, he wished his friends would give it a rest! How many times did he have to tell them he'd find his own women.

An ice show?

THE NIGHT STARTED OFF bad. Then it got worse.

Craig's heart wasn't in the impromptu date.

Two blocks away from the stadium, a petite brunette, Gina, checked her watch for the fifth time. "We're going to be late."

"Not much. We'll be there by the start of the first act." Craig smiled reassuringly. "Relax."

The skaters were finishing their warm-ups as Craig directed Gina to their seats. Five minutes into the performance, the lights went out.

A communal groan signaled everyone's annoyance. Gina's was the loudest.

The announcer came on ten minutes later. "Ladies and gentlemen," he said, "we apologize for our technical problems, but the main transformer has blown. I'm sorry, but there's nothing we can do to salvage tonight's performance—"

The audience groaned again.

"Everyone will receive tickets for a rescheduled performance. Again, we apologize. Thank you for your understanding and cooperation."

"Can you believe this?" Gina fumed. "We fought traffic for an hour to get here and the performance is canceled?"

Craig was used to delays. He'd try to salvage the evening as best he could. "These things happen. Are you hungry? We could go to Nickerson's and have a piece of their lemon meringue pie."

"I'm on a diet."

"Then how about a cappuccino at Mansfield's?"

"If I drank a cappuccino at this hour, I'd be wired for the night," she said, pouting. "I wanted to see the ice show."

Everyone got to their feet and gathered their things, complaining lightly.

"I'll get in line for the tickets," Craig said. "It'll take a few minutes, judging by the size of the crowd. Why don't you wait in the lobby?"

"This burns me. Really burns me." She jerked at the handle of her purse that had somehow become entangled in her coat. "How can they do this? Do they think people have nothing better to do than come back for a performance another night? People made plans. Haven't they heard of repairmen? Can't they call a repairman?"

"I'll get in line," he said. "It shouldn't take long.

Gina sighed sanctimoniously. "I might as well wait with you."

Great, he thought. He'd been hoping for a break from her complaining.

The line moved too slowly for her.

She tapped her acrylic nails on her purse impatiently. "Listen, I'm going to the lobby and see what's taking so long."

"That's not necessary," he told her. "The line's moving. Let's just wait our turn."

"It'll take all night if somebody doesn't do something."

Clearly, she thought he should. Before he could stop her, Gina marched to the front of the line and pushed her way into the lobby.

Stepping out of line, Craig went to look for Gina.

"I'm telling you, Bozo—"

She had the manager cornered, tapping him in the middle of the chest with long, bloodred nails.

"We want a cash refund!"

"Ma'am, we're not allowed to do that," the manager said.

"Yeah? Well, I don't intend to budge an inch until you give everyone their money back. I'll tie up the line all night if I have to! Refuse, Mr. Hotshot, and I'll call my attorney. Then we'll see how fast your policy changes!"

"Gina, please," Craig said. "There's no need to make a scene."

Suddenly, her finely chiseled profile reminded him of a ferret.

Just then, a man in the lineup called to another. "If that loudmouth broad gets her way, we'll all get our money back."

Craig was appalled to realize the crowd was actually pulling for her.

"Ma'am, I'm sorry," the manager said. "I'm authorized by the company to offer tickets for another performance only."

Craig felt sorry for the guy. He looked like a trapped animal struggling to hold his ground against the ferret.

Gina turned up the volume. "You're trying to cheat us! How dare you try to cheat us this way! We came all the way downtown to see this performance and there isn't going to be one." She pinned him with an evil ferret look. "You give us back our money, you hear? It's only fair that you return our money."

She stepped closer.

"Ma'am." The manager straightened a little. "I'm afraid that if you don't move on, I'll have to call security."

Gina's upper lip curled with contempt. "You just try it, Bub."

"Ma'am—"

"You messed up. You inconvenienced us!" She turned to him. "Craig! Make him give us our money back, right now!"

"Look, sir," Craig said, just wanting to get Gina out of there without creating more of a problem. "Is there any way you can return the money? If you can do that, we'll be on our way."

"It's against policy," the man repeated.

"I understand, but the lady is upset—"

The manager held his ground. "No money refunded. Just tickets. And you both have to leave. Immediately."

"He can't talk to us like that—" Now Gina was beginning to sound as shrill as a hyena. "You can't talk to us like that. Who's your boss? Get him out here. I'll show you that you can't treat paying customers this way!"

The manager motioned for Craig and Gina to move on.

She was still yelling that they'd been cheated as Craig dragged her out of the auditorium. He was certain he'd spotted a Sparrow employee standing in line, witnessing the whole scene.

Gina dug in her heels as Craig dragged her through the lobby. "We'll march right back in there and straighten this out. He can't get away with this!"

"Gina, there's no way in hell I'm going back in there!"

"Well, I am. I paid good money for those tickets and we're not about to be ripped off." She started back inside. "I'm not being nice this time. Bonehead is going to get a piece of my mind!"

Exasperated, Craig watched her stride briskly back into the building. He'd never abandoned a date in his life, but for Gina, he'd make an exception.

4

"NUTS?"

Nuts to you, Temple thought when a middle-aged executive tried a tired line on her.

Working her way down the narrow aisle, Temple served peanuts, coffee, juice and complimentary papers to twenty-two passengers, then started the round again.

When she'd first applied for flight school, she had thought being a flight attendant was a glamorous profession. Boy, was that ever a misconception. Most of her eighty hours a month in the air were spent on foot working at top speed. Glamorous lasted only during the walk across the terminal—everything before and after was plain hard work.

Factor in reams of reports to complete—on minor medications given to passengers, lost-and-found articles, equipment that needed attention and numerous other matters, and glamour became exhaustion.

Certainly no one had ever told her that a 6:00 a.m. flight meant she had to report for preflight at five, which meant getting up at 3:45 a.m., at the latest.

She had been lucky, though, in having the early-morning flight as an almost permanent assignment, with only an occasional schedule change for weekends and holidays. The hard work and lack of glamour notwithstanding, she loved the job.

This morning, however, might be an exception. Craig and Scotty had the plane tilted at an angle that, though imperceptible to the passengers, made it tough, if not impossible, to bulldoze the refreshment cart up the aisle. They were probably thoroughly enjoying their little joke at her expense. Just wait till they got their coffee.

There was only a little under an hour between flights, making the day seem unusually long and tedious. A long soak in a Jacuzzi and a quiet night was sounding more and more tempting.

Preparing to depart Memphis at 3:10 on the return flight, Temple slid the flight-attendant seat sideways then pulled the passenger door closed and locked it.

Taking her seat, she fastened her seat belt, smiling at the passengers in the front row. As the plane taxied to the runway for departure, the flight-attendant call light started flashing repeatedly. After four false calls, Temple switched on the intercom.

"Will the child in 12-C please stop playing with the flight-attendant call button? Thank you."

During takeoff, the child vented his rage by screaming at the top of his lungs.

I love my job. I love my job. I love my job, she repeated silently.

The final flight of the day was wonderfully quiet. The passengers either slept or read. Still, by the time the plane touched down in Dallas, Temple was glad to sign out.

She was leaving the terminal, looking forward to that long soak in the Jacuzzi when Scotty caught up with her.

"Hey, Temple, girl." He fell into step beside her. "Small hitch in the dinner plans tonight."

Darn! She'd forgotten the "dinner plans." "Oh, brother." She hated to think what the small hitch was.

"I invited Jon Bennett to join us—"

"Scotty—"

"Come on, Temple. I told Stephanie you didn't want to be set up again, but she thinks you and Jon just might hit it off," he said. "I know. Blind dates are the pits. But how else are you going to rotate stock?"

She stopped short. "Rotate stock?"

"Aw, you know what I mean. How are you going to find 'the one' if you don't look? Come on, be a sport."

Sighing, Temple accepted the inevitable. "Okay, who's this Jon Bennett? Separated, divorced, desperate? What?"

"We haven't known him long. Met him a couple of weeks ago at a friend's house. Seems to be interesting enough. Works for the telephone company. A little shy around women, but you'll have no trouble talking to him."

So far so good.

"What's the hitch?"

"Jon called Steph and wondered if you could pick him up. His car's in the garage."

"In the garage?"

"That's what he said."

"Couldn't he take a cab?"

"I guess, but what's it going to hurt if you pick him up? It's right on the way."

"I don't know, Scotty..."

"Seven? And be prompt. Steph gets bent out of shape when the roast is dry."

"How do I get into these things?" she said, exasperated.

"Just pick him up...you really don't mind, do you?"

"I guess not. If you think he's trustworthy. He is, isn't he?"

"Seemed so."

"Okay, I'll pick him up." *Why did they sound like words of doom?*

"Great. Look, he's funny, interesting. Definitely not boring, just a little shy."

"So you said," she murmured warily.

When they stopped beside her truck, she noticed that Craig's parking spot was empty. She felt a little disappointed that he hadn't wasted any time leaving the terminal.

"You don't have to sell me on him," she said. "It's only dinner, not a lifetime commitment."

Scotty looked relieved. "Thanks, you're a sport."

"Just keep in mind that if this guy's a flake, your insurance better be paid."

"Would I steer you wrong?"

"Don't pull your act with me, Scotty, me boy. You're one terrific pilot, but your record as a matchmaker stinks. I still haven't forgotten Luc Carter."

His hands flipped palms up in mock surrender. "Hey, I had no idea that was prison pallor!"

"Does the phrase, 'Check it out' mean anything to you? Jon had better be a little higher caliber."

"I resent that remark."

"I mean that remark."

"Like I said— Save the cynicism until you've spent a little time with him," Scotty advised. "After all, this could be Mr. Remarkable."

Temple sighed again. Remarkable. *Ha! It'll be remarkable if it's a normal date.* Using the back of a brochure, she wrote down the address Scotty gave her.

"Tell him I'll pick him up around six, okay?"

"Six is fine."

HOLDING THE PHONE between her ear and shoulder, Temple propped her feet up on the coffee table and studied the polish on her toenails.

"No, honest, Grams. I have a date.

"His name is Jon Bennett.

"No, Darrell didn't work out.

"We just didn't click.

"I have no idea what Jon's financial situation is. I haven't met him yet.

"No, he's not a perfect stranger." She could nearly promise he wasn't a perfect anything. "He's an acquaintance of Jim and Stephanie Scott.

"Jim Scott, Grams. Scotty, the first officer I fly with—

"No, Jim wouldn't set me up with a pervert—

"No, I'm sure he's harmless.

"I don't know why he isn't married. Maybe he has been—

"I'll ask to see the divorce papers before he gets into the truck."

Temple had to grin at Grams's nonstop questions.

"Scotty's already married, Grams. To Stephanie.

"He was married to Stephanie before I met him, Grams.

"No, that's Craig Stevens.

"Yes, Helen and Frank's boy." Temple twirled the telephone cord around her finger, anticipating the next question.

"No, Grams, he isn't married.

"Of course not! Just because a guy isn't married doesn't mean that he's—"

She anticipated the next question.

"We're just friends.

"Because that's the way we both want it.

"Well, I'm sure he wants to...some day. But not to me.

"He's a pilot, Grams. You know I don't date pilots.

"Dad has nothing to do with that decision. I like to keep work and play separate."

Grams had questioned her about her aversion to pilots before, but she was sure there was no subconscious correlation between that and her choice of profession.

"Yes, I will.

"Yes. I promise.

"Grams, please stop worrying.

"Yes, I will. I promise. Geez, look at the time. Don't you have choir rehearsal tonight?

"Yes, I'll call you Sunday."

Hanging up, Temple pressed a sofa pillow to her face. *"Aaaggghhh!"*

AWARE THAT Scotty and Stephanie liked informal dinners, Temple wore a pair of white silk pants and a pale green silk shirt. Blow-drying her hair, she decided she liked the new cut. It was bouncy and casual, easy to take care of. A nice change.

Making a moue in the mirror, she mouthed the words *hot, hot, hot.* With a touch of mascara to lashes that defined sherry-brown eyes, she gave her appearance a last once-over, blew herself a kiss and switched off the light.

The address Scotty had given her wasn't familiar, but she found it easily. Though well past its prime, it was a nice enough area.

The building was an elegant old brownstone. A black wrought-iron gate opened easily to her touch and led through a small garden. Double doors with frosted glass opened into a tastefully decorated foyer. But there the elegance ended. The carpet was a stained, unsanitary green. Beige walls blended into obscurity. The only redeeming feature was the carved oak stairway that even time and lack of care had failed to alter.

Moving to the desk, she gave the security guard her name. Within a few minutes, a man descended the stairway.

Tall and painfully thin, he looked to be several years her senior. He was wearing sedate khaki trousers, a white golf shirt and leather loafers. His glasses were wider than his face.

Summoning a smile, Temple said. "Jon?"

Color flooded the man's pale features, making his ears stand out from his crewcut like two, giant hydrangeas.

An alarm went off in her head. *Uh-oh.*

"Hello," he said.

His voice was so inaudible she'd barely made out the greeting.

Temple extended her hand. "Temple Burney."

"Nicetomeetyou."

Unbelievable! A mumbler. Megaphone Darrell on Saturday, Jon the Mumbler tonight. She was batting an even thousand this week.

"Ready to go?" she asked.

"Thank you. Yes," he whispered.

Experience told her disaster loomed, but being a trooper she led the way out to the truck. After all, Steph and Scotty were expecting them, and while she wouldn't hesitate to call Scotty and bail out, she didn't want to waste the efforts Steph was sure to have made toward a nice evening.

As they pulled away from the curb, she said. "Hope you don't mind the truck. I've driven it so long I can't bear to part with it."

"Idon'tmind."

"Pardon?" He was mumbling again.

"Idon'tmind."

It sounded to her as if he'd said, "You've lost your mind." Obviously not. Scotty had said Jon was shy, not insensitive. Maybe things would improve when he relaxed. At the moment, he was plastered against the passenger door.

Picking up speed on the freeway, she tried to keep the conversation rolling. "So, you're a friend of Scotty and Steph?"

"Yes."

"Pardon?"

"Yes."

"Very long?"

"Notvery."

She turned. "Pardon?"

His eyes darted back and forth in an attempt to avoid hers, reminding her of a lizard. A great big old lizard. A trapped lizard, dying to get loose.

"Not very long. Watch that car. It's coming over." Jon collapsed on his seat, wiping sweat from his forehead. His superhuman effort at normal conversation had clearly exhausted him.

Mentally sighing, Temple concentrated on driving. It was going to be a long night.

Thirty minutes later, they exited the freeway and entered a pretty, tree-lined residential area. The homes were mid-priced, brick, with small lawns and colorful flower-bordered walks.

The smell of outdoor barbecue flavored the air as Temple drove the Silverado to Scotty and Steph's cul-de-sac. Temple parked at the curb, between two abandoned children's bicycles and a Big Wheel. Jon followed her silently to the door, like a shadow.

Jim Scott, I'm going to throttle you.

Scotty met them at the door, beaming like a proud father. "Come in! How's it going?"

Temple slammed her purse in his stomach as she walked by. "I'm going to get you for this, Jimbo," she promised under her breath.

Recovering from the blow, Scotty frowned at her, then greeted Jon. "How's it going, buddy?"

"Fine, thank you." Jon managed a loud whisper.

Scotty's two older children burst from their bedrooms, running down the hallway to greet the new arrivals. Temple hugged the boisterous kids. Pete was a miniature version of Scotty, while Cari had Steph's delicate features.

Scotty introduced Jon, then told the children to go watch videos in the den. They ran off in a flurry of excited chatter, Cari dragging a "blankee" behind her.

Steph appeared in the kitchen doorway, holding the baby. A diaper was draped over her shoulder to catch stray dribbles. "Hi, guys!"

"Hi, Steph." Temple hugged her friend and the baby together, not resisting the urge to cup the infant's head with her hand.

"Hello," Jon whispered.

"Dinner's almost ready," Stephanie said. "Scotty, fix Temple and Jon a drink."

"What'll it be, guys?" Scotty moved to the liquor cabinet to drop ice cubes into glasses.

"Just Perrier for me," Temple said.

"Jon?"

"Whateveryou'rehaving."

"Pardon?"

"Whateveryou'rehaving."

Scotty glanced questioningly at Temple.

She shrugged. She didn't know what he'd said.

Pouring Scotch into a glass, Scotty added water and handed it to Jon.

"So, how's business at the telephone company?"

"Good."

Temple and Scotty both smiled at having understood Jon's answer. Scotty decided to be brave, "Keeping busy, huh?"

"Yes, thestormtheothernightdownedseverallines. Iwasoutallnight. Ican'tgetrestedup."

Temple and Scotty turned, saying simultaneously, "What?"

Steph reappeared, carrying her sleeping baby. "I'm going to put her to bed, then we'll eat." She wrinkled her nose. "Teething time again."

Temple stood up to help. "Can I help?"

"No, no, you and Jon sit there and get to know each other," she sang out as she carried the baby down the hallway.

That escape route effectively cut off, Temple sank back onto the sofa. Her eyes inadvertently met Jon's. Flushing a deep red, he quickly looked away. *He's getting worse, not better. The evening is going to be endless.*

Dinner was a disaster. Steph's lovely standing rib roast was lost in a sea of awkwardness as the four tried to carry on a stilted conversation. Temple was horrified when she realized she chewed louder than Jon talked.

Jon mumbled something again, and Steph, Scotty and Temple leaned forward in an effort to make out what he was saying.

It was hopeless. It sounded like, "A brick wall shit in a water pail," but it couldn't have been.

Smiling, they nodded their heads, pretending to understand when in fact they hadn't a clue what he'd said.

Once, it sounded as if he'd said, "Grandmother was a hooker," but Temple had to believe she was mistaken.

She could see Jon thought they were all stone-deaf and had severely limited vocabularies.

"Huh? Excuse me? What?" was repeated so many times during the meal, Temple was embarrassed. Before dessert, she was so frustrated she wanted to throttle him and choke out the words!

"Really, your dog was hit by a car?" Steph asked once.

"No, Idon'thaveadog. IsaidIgotanewsetoftires," he said.

"That's so sad." They all nodded, agreeing that the loss of one's pet was traumatic.

"We had a dog once," Steph said. "But it got old and we had to put him to sleep." She sighed. "The hardest thing we ever had to do. I can't imagine losing one in an accident. It must have been horrible."

"Did you have a service for it? Pet owners do that now," Scotty said. "There's a pet cemetery not far from here."

"Igotanewsetoftires. Idon'thaveadog," Jon repeated.

"Well, I doubt that I would, either, but a pet does become an integral part of the family," Scotty conceded.

"They'regoodtires. Goodyearmakesthem."

"Goodyear Blimp? No, never seen it. How about you, Steph, Temple?"

Temple shook her head, wiping her mouth with a napkin. "No, never saw it."

"Me neither, but I'd like to," Steph offered. "Some friends of ours have. They passed by it on the way to Orlando last year. Dessert, anyone?"

She served cake and coffee in the living room. By now, Temple had a throbbing headache.

The mumble suggested they leave around nine—or that's what she hoped he'd said because she immediately got up and started for the door.

"The dinner was wonderful," she complimented Steph.

"Thanks. Listen, I want you and Jon to take a piece of cake home with you. Come in the kitchen a sec while I wrap it up for you."

Jon said something that sounded like "Blow your head off if you do," but Temple followed Steph into the kitchen on the assumption he'd said something closer to "That's very nice of you."

She didn't know. She hadn't understood a word he'd said all evening. Even Darrell looked good to her right now.

"Ye gads!" Steph whispered as the door closed behind them. "Guess this means you won't be seeing him again."

"Not likely."

"I'm so sorry. I had no idea he was a mumbler."

"It's all right," Temple said, her frustration softening. "He seems very nice."

"Maybe, but I didn't understand a word he said!"

"Me neither. No telling what we talked about."

Steph nodded pensively. "I hope we didn't agree to do this again."

Temple couldn't help laughing at the apprehension on her friend's face.

Around nine-thirty, Temple dropped Jon off at his apartment house. He stood, cake in hand, looking rather forlorn at the failed evening.

"Thankyou. Ihadanicetime."

"Pardon?"

"Ihadanicetime. Thankyou."

Temple nodded, smiling. "Sorry about your dog." Shifting into gear, she drove off.

Glancing in the rearview mirror, she saw Jon still standing in front of the gate as she merged into traffic.

What she couldn't hear was Jon mumbling, "I don't have a dog. I said, TIRES. Are you guys deaf, or something?"

5

"I KNOW WHAT the problem is," Temple announced.

Craig sipped his coffee. "I didn't know we had a problem."

Mechanical trouble had temporarily grounded their plane. Temple and Craig were waiting in the lunchroom for word on whether the flight would be rescheduled.

"I'm serious. I've been thinking a lot about this."

"Okay. I'll bite. What's our problem?" Craig stirred sugar into his coffee.

"It's the blind dates. We're doing it all wrong." Temple couldn't stand one more Jon Bennett or Darrell... Darrell... Damn! What was that man's last name?

"There's a right way and a wrong way to date?" Craig asked.

"There has to be. And I must be doing it wrong. I couldn't meet this many losers otherwise."

"Hey, give Scotty a little credit for some of those."

Temple shook her head slowly in disbelief. "Last night was a nightmare. All the man wanted to do was talk about his dead dog."

Craig studied her over the rim of his cup. "So, I suppose you've come up with a solution to this problem of ours?"

"It's so simple." She set down her cup. "Who knows me better than anyone? And who knows you like an open book?"

"No one."

"Wrong. Think."

"I suppose this is where I say I know you better than anyone else?"

He did. And the more she thought about her plan, the more certain she was it would work.

"Well, isn't it true?"

Craig shrugged.

"So, from now on," she told him, "I'll arrange dates for you with my friends and you can do the same for me."

His coffee cup paused halfway to his mouth. "I thought we both agreed. We're not good at this dating thing."

"But this is different," she insisted. "I know you'd never set me up with a loser, and I certainly wouldn't suggest someone I didn't think was right for you. I'd want you to have a good time. And you'd want the same for me." She leaned toward him, excited about her new plan. "Think about it, Craig. Our dates would be prescreened, so to speak. No more dates from hell."

No more shouters, ex-cons or mumblers.

"See the advantages?" she said.

"No." He drained his coffee cup and signaled for the waitress.

"Craig, it's the perfect solution. We've known each other forever—or certainly long enough to know each other's preferences in the opposite sex. And we definitely know what the other doesn't like."

She could see he still wasn't convinced.

"Temple, you're far more concerned about this than I am," he said. "How many times do I have to repeat myself? I like my life the way it is. If you want to marry me, then we'll talk. Otherwise, I'll do my own PR, if you don't mind."

His statement took her completely by surprise. The mere thought of her marrying him sent her pulse rate into double time. He was kidding, of course, but wow! Her fantasies could really take off on this one!

"I'll marry you," she bantered. "I didn't realized you'd asked."

For the briefest of moments, their gazes met. Holding her breath, she waited for him to retract the offer with some silly mock countersuggestion. But he didn't.

"Maybe you haven't been listening," he said quietly.

"What?"

His glance shifted away. "Go on with your plan. I'm listening."

Momentarily shaken, she had to reorganize her thoughts. "Your dates have been as insane as mine. I—I want you to meet someone who'll make you happy—look after you."

Craig studied the bottom of his coffee cup as if considering her idea.

"Exactly what are you looking for in a man, Temple?"

"What every woman looks for. Someone who's kind, sensitive, caring, loves animals and small children."

Someone who talks normally and doesn't like marine aquariums.

"All that and be a man, too? Wow."

"It's possible."

He leaned back in the booth and stretched his arms along the back of the bench. "Well, I'm not in the market for a screening program. I'm capable of finding a woman for myself."

Ignoring him, she sipped her coffee. "We'll start with Gabrielle."

"Nuh-uh. If I have to go along with this crazy idea, we'll start with Bill."

"Gabrielle. She's perfect for you. Fun, outgoing—"

"Bill's caring, sensitive—"

"Gabrielle Nielson. You remember her. She was one of my roomies in flight school?"

She wouldn't mention the other one—Nancy Johnson.

"Gabrielle's nice, Craig. Laid-back, comfortable. Loves children and animals. You'll like her." She paused for a moment, then said, "Let me see what she's doing Saturday night. You two have so much in common! She works for TWA. If she's not working an overnighter, I know she'll want to—"

"No," Craig interrupted. "I want to know what I'm getting into before I ring that doorbell—"

"Of course. I'll phone her right now."

"Temple, if you want me to do something Saturday night, you come by the apartment and we'll grill a couple of steaks, watch a movie, kick back and relax—"

But Temple was already headed for the row of telephones lining the lobby wall. She was back in ten minutes, grinning from ear to ear.

"Temple, I'm doing this, okay, but not because I want to meet this woman! Only to show you this idea won't work."

She ignored his tone. "You'll love her. Trust me!"

RETYING HIS TIE and adjusting it up close, Craig studied his reflection in the mirror. He didn't feel good about this surefire plan of Temple's. Why hadn't he insisted that she come by instead? If she didn't want to cook steaks, they could have ordered in Chinese. She'd said she wasn't doing anything, and experience told him he would enjoy her company far more than Gabrielle's even if the woman was gorgeous and charming. Truth was, Temple had spoiled him for any other woman, but she had no idea.

Her blind spot about pilots kept her from recognizing how great they could be together. So, until she got over this notion about not mixing her private life with her career, he just had to take it easy and go along with this crazy idea of hers.

Jerking the knot in the tie free, he tossed it onto the bed in frustration. When was he going to learn to say no? Such a simple word. Two letters, easy to say. No.

N.O.

No.

NO. NO!

So simple, and yet he couldn't say it to Temple.

Staring at his image in the mirror, he thought about the slip he'd made with her. Had he actually asked her to marry him?

No. No way.

"I'll marry you. I didn't realize you'd asked." Her words came back to him like a rushing wind.

Was she kidding, or was she testing the waters?

Could she have been serious?

Come on, Craig. Where's your head! It was a joke!

At precisely 7:25, Craig parked the Lincoln in front of Gabrielle's apartment building. Glancing up at the second story, he drew a breath of resignation. A few minutes later, he rang the doorbell and waited, glancing up and down the wide hallway. Not great, but nice.

When the door opened, Craig's interest was piqued. Gabrielle was actually pretty. Blond curls framed a gamine face, and bright blue eyes sparkled back at him. The mix of hot-pink jeans, painted red toenails in sling-back sandals and a chartreuse tank top was cute.

"Craig Stevens," he said. "Temple's friend?"

"Hi. Gabrielle." She giggled. "Temple's friend, too." With a grand sweep of her hand, she invited him in. "En-trée."

Craig stepped inside, smiling.

"Parlez-vous français?"

He knew just enough French to know he couldn't speak it. "Very little. Are you French?"

"No, but I'm in Europe a lot. Let me take your jacket."

He shrugged out of his coat, and handed it to her, now acutely aware of an odor that was beginning to make him slightly nauseated.

"Want a beer?"

"Sure."

He caught a movement from the corner of his eye. A long, gray cat crept along the baseboard, an evil look in its yellow eyes as it measured him up and down with a Garfield look of disdain. He wasn't an animal person.

"Your cat?"

Gabrielle's voice came from the depths of the refrigerator. "One of them. I have five." She shut the refrigerator door with her foot. "It's difficult in an apartment, but cats are really good about taking care of themselves. You don't smell my litter boxes, do you?"

"Uh, no," he lied. Litter boxes. His stomach rolled.

"I didn't think so. Do you like cats?"

"Actually, I don't know much about them."

"You didn't have one as a child?"

"No." Not likely to have one as an adult, either. Certainly not five.

"A dog?"

"No."

"Oh. Light beer okay?"

"Fine."

He followed her back to the living area where she gestured for him to sit down. *"Asseyez-vous."*

He perched on the edge of the couch, edging back a fraction when he noticed a yellow feline resembling a tacky fur neck-piece curved around the leg of the coffee table.

"You really should get a cat," Gabrielle said. "They're lots of company, and they do virtually take care of themselves."

"I don't have the time to give to a pet. I'm gone a lot."

She brightened. "Yeah, Temple said you work out of Dallas/Fort Worth, too. It's a wonder we haven't bumped into each other before."

Gabrielle sank onto the floor and pulled another motley yellow cat into her lap. One eye fixed on him with a challenging look, while the other free-floated.

"How is Temple, anyway?"

Craig shifted, counting cats. "You haven't seen her lately?" If Temple had fixed him up with someone she didn't know very well, he'd strangle her.

"Not lately. I fly international flights—Paris, mostly. We only talked for a moment when she called about us meeting. How's she getting along?"

"Fine."

Casually leaning back, Craig crossed his leg, then jumped, almost spilling his beer. Something furry had attached itself to his thigh.

With a glance at Gabrielle, he attempted to brush it away but was disgusted to find it stuck to his moist hand. Visions of an alien creature from "The X-Files" flashed through his mind. With his luck, it would permanently attach itself to him, growing until it devoured him completely. On closer inspection, Craig identified the thing as a huge fur ball.

He balanced the beer in one hand, and covertly tried to wipe the clinging hair ball onto the edge of the sofa.

"Oh, gosh!" Gabrielle cried, setting aside her beer. "I'm sorry. My chow is shedding."

His stomach sank. "You have dogs, too?"

"Just two." She plucked at the collection of fur he'd gathered on his trousers. "A chow and a rottweiler. My dog walker took the boys out earlier for a run in the park."

Managing to extricate himself from the tentacles of the fur ball, he set the beer on the end of the coffee table and tried to dry his hands on his trousers. Clearly nonplussed, Gabrielle rubbed moisture from her beer can, dampened the hair ball into a roll and arced it toward an already over-flowing wastebasket.

Forcing himself to relax, Craig smiled.

She smiled back.

As the silence stretched, Craig's mind cast about for something, anything, to say. "So, you and Temple were in flight school together—"

"Roommates. Temple and Nancy and I were real close back then. Nancy stayed in Virginia, but I was really glad when Temple and I were both assigned to Dallas. She said you've been friends nearly all your lives. You must have met Nancy."

"Nancy?" His smile faded.

"Yeah. Nancy Johnson. She and Temple were best buddies. I know you must have met her."

"Um, yes, I met her." For a moment, the smell of Prep-aration H and bananas overode the smell of the litter boxes. The memory made his stomach cramp.

"Temple's the best." Gabrielle rubbed the ears of the yellow cat who'd unwrapped itself from the leg of the cof-fee table. "I don't understand why she hasn't married. Guys are crazy about her. How old is she now? Thirty-two?"

"Thirty-one. Her birthday's in December."

"Oh, yeah. Christmas baby. Is she still dating that guy?"

"Guy?" He frowned. "She's never mentioned a 'Guy.'"

"You know, that guy, Steve. She thought he'd be the one, you know. I mean 'the one'?" she said with emphasis. "Maybe you didn't meet him. That was a while back. She was irritated with herself for being so gullible she probably never talked about it."

Following her conversation was like keeping up with a bouncing rubber ball.

She grinned. "Steve worked in a fish restaurant. Told her he owned it. Then she found out he was feeding her a line." Gabrielle giggled. "Line. Feeding her? Get it?"

Craig smiled obligingly. "Oh . . . *that* Steve."

It bothered him that he hadn't known about Steve. He thought Temple told him everything. Apparently not.

"Actually, I guess I'd be surprised if she did talk about him. She was screaming mad about the whole thing. You ever lie to a woman?"

"Excuse me?"

"Lie, like Steve did to Temple."

"I try not to." Unless, of course, they ask about something like did he notice an eye-watering odor in the apartment.

"Not even a white lie?"

"No."

"Well, then here's to the first honest man I've ever met. *Salut.*" She lifted her beer to him.

He lifted his can to her, ready to sip a salute when three more felines entered from the kitchen, tails in the air, marching along behind one another like cartoon figures.

Leaping onto the arm of the couch, they moved in silent rhythm, trailing along behind him on the back of the sofa.

Lying down, they stretched out, nose to tail. The paws of the middle one slipped around his neck, forming a collar just beneath his ears.

He brushed a hand over his hair, hoping to discourage the animal. It didn't work. The cat leaned forward to smell his hair, then nudged Craig with its nose. Its hot breath on his scalp made his skin crawl. He suppressed a shiver as well as the desire to scratch his nose.

"Nice cats."

"Aren't they?"

"And you've got two dogs?" His skin was beginning to itch.

"Yes, Harry and David. I just love their products, don't you?"

He ducked the amorous cat again. "Excuse me?"

"You know, Harry and David? I get these wonderful catalogs through the mail? They make sinfully delicious cheesecakes. That's where I got the idea for the dogs' names. Harry and David."

"Oh." The woman was nuts.

He was rescued from further comment when the front door opened and a large red chow straining against a heavy leash leaped in, followed by a more sedate rottweiler whose challenging gaze locked on Craig. The teenage girl who'd walked the dogs unsnapped their leashes and disappeared into the kitchen.

The chow zeroed in on Craig, sniffing at his pants cuff, then rubbed against his leg, leaving a thick layer of red hair from knee to hem. Craig moved over slightly.

Gabrielle grabbed the chow's collar as it began sniffing Craig's shoe with more determination. "No, no, Harry."

She smiled apologetically. "He's very proprietary. Sometimes he marks his territory." So far, the rottweiler had contented itself with standing guard at the corner of the coffee table.

Pulling from Gabrielle's grasp, the chow leaped up and planted its paws on Craig's shirtfront.

Gabrielle relaxed back into her chair, beaming like a proud parent. "Harry likes you."

Any response Craig might have made was wiped away by the dog's tongue as it washed his face. Trying to avoid the animal's wet licks, Craig's head smacked against the back of the sofa, sending up a cloud of cat hair.

Gabrielle continued to smile. "You're wonderful with animals. You really should get a pet."

Craig was fending off the aggressive dog with his forearm, when the teenager slouched out of the kitchen with a sandwich in one hand and a can of soda in the other. "Later, dude."

The door had hardly closed behind her when the doorbell rang.

Gabrielle popped up like a jack-in-the-box. "That must be the ribs. Hope you don't mind that I didn't cook. I'm not very good at it."

She went to the door while Craig elbowed away the chow and moved to the edge of the couch in an attempt to keep the cats out of his hair. He wanted to leave, but he stayed because Gabrielle was Temple's friend. He couldn't see how they'd maintained any kind of friendship. Temple's apartment was always clean, fresh, smelling faintly of vanilla. He felt comfortable there. So what was he doing here?

A gangly teen in an embroidered ball cap stood angled in the doorway. "Smokey's Bar-B-Q."

"Where have you been? I was beginning to think you weren't coming."

"Sorry. Had trouble finding the address."

Gabrielle flipped open the cardboard box. "Geez, they're cold!"

"Half price 'cause I was late. Traffic."

Craig escaped the cats and took the box from Gabrielle. He didn't intend to have this turn into another Gina fiasco.

"How much?"

"Twelve-fifty."

Craig handed him fifteen dollars, and shut the door.

Gabrielle took back the box.

"They're cold as ice. I'll reheat them." She carried the food into the kitchen. "Want another beer?"

"Thanks, I'll finish the one I have."

He tripped over a cat on his way back to the sofa. Stumbling, he caught himself, cracking his shin on the coffee table. He sank onto the edge of the couch, swallowing an expression his mother would have disapproved of. The rottweiler, looking unperturbed by his agony, licked its chops, cold black eyes observing him implacably. Gabrielle was in the kitchen. No help if the dog decided to go for his jugular vein.

"Mind if I wash my hands?"

"Through the bedroom," Gabrielle called back. "First door on the right."

Gingerly pushing open the bedroom door, he stopped short. Clothes were strung over the bed, draped from doorknobs and the backs of chairs. The tight quarters resembled a large, messy closet. How had Temple lived with this?

At least the bed was made, but depressions in the thick comforter made it clear that the cats considered it their bed.

He found the bathroom, more by smell than observation, and flipped on the light. A large inky-black cat, green eyes gleaming like coals, was curled in the sink. The feline did not appear inclined to move.

"Just push Satan out of the sink," Gabrielle called from the living room. "He thinks it's his. The porcelain feels good against his tummy, I guess."

Craig's eyes stung and his nose burned from the pungent odor in the room. He deposited the cat on the floor and turned on the water. After rinsing his hands, he picked up a fairly fresh towel and spotted the source of the smell. Three litter boxes sat on the floor of the closet.

As he left the bedroom, the smell of burning cardboard wafted to him, nearly overriding the stench of the litter boxes. When Craig entered the kitchen, Gabrielle was pouring cat food into five dishes lined up on newspaper in a corner.

"What's burning?"

"Oh, darn!"

Smoke was seeping out around the oven door.

Grabbing a hot pad, Craig jerked open the oven door, leaning back to evade the rolling cloud of black smoke that billowed out.

"Got an extinguisher?"

"No!" Her hands fluttered helplessly in the air, stirring the smoke.

"Damn," he muttered.

Yanking out the oven rack, he grabbed a damp dishcloth that was draped over a burner and beat out the flaming box.

"Oh, geez-Louise, will you look at that," Gabrielle wailed, peering over his shoulder.

"You're supposed to take the ribs out of the box before you heat them," he told her.

Her eyebrows shot up as she surveyed the mess. "No kidding?"

Craig headed for the bathroom again. *Ten minutes and I'm out of here. Fifteen tops. And then, Burney, you're going to pay for this one. Big time.*

Craig quickly washed his hands while Satan eyed him warily from the open closet door.

As he was drying off, he spotted Gabrielle's curling iron on the counter, the frayed cord plugged in, the barrel smoldering amid at least thirty bottles of cosmetics that littered the tiny counter.

"Did you know your curling iron's on?" he called. *And obviously has been since early this morning?*

"Again? Where is my brain! I forget to turn it off. Mind unplugging it for me?"

Fearing electrocution, Craig gingerly reached around the blistering hot barrel and knocked the hot plug out of the socket. The cord knocked over a bottle of perfume. Grabbing at it, he started a landslide of hair spray, styling gel, deodorant and a bottle of mouthwash that fell in a domino effect, clattering noisily to the floor. A container of aspirin crashed to the floor where its contents spilled across the black and green tiles.

Damn.

Satan shot out of the closet like a bullet, smacking into the bathroom wall and ricocheting off it into the door frame, nearly shutting his own tail in the door as he finally shot through it. A harrowing screech from the other side signaled the sideswipe of at least one other feline.

"What was that?" Gabrielle called from the kitchen.

"Nothing. Be right there."

The cockeyed yellow cat sauntered in to investigate the melee and immediately began eating the scattered aspirin.

"Stop that!" Craig muttered, grabbing it. He fished two pills out of the cat's mouth and flushed them down the toilet. Cockeyed wasn't at all happy about the operation and took a mean swipe at Craig before being pitched into the bedroom.

Dropping to his hands and knees, Craig scraped together the remainder of the aspirin, separating cat hairs from the tablets as best he could, and stuffed the pills back into the bottle. Retrieving the cosmetics, Craig piled perfume, hair spray, styling gel, deodorant and mouthwash back onto the counter. He doubted Gabrielle would notice the difference.

He returned to the living room, the telltale scent of Giorgio clinging to him. "Leaving your curling iron on is dangerous."

She sniffed, looking at him with a slight frown.

Did she think he had been into her perfume?

He started to explain, but she interrupted. "You some kind of safety nut?"

"No, but that's a damn good way to set the place on fire."

She flipped the last of the ribs from the scorched box onto a plate.

"You can buy curling irons that automatically shut themselves off," he added.

"I've had that one since high school. I don't want to break in a new one." She smiled reassuringly. "Don't worry. I leave it on all the time. Dinner's ready."

His soda can had cat hair coating the sides.

Brushing away what he could without being obvious, he took a tentative sip. Gabrielle picked up a cat from the floor.

She held it on her lap while she ate, feeding it and the four other felines tidbits from her plate.

"It's not bad, is it?" she tossed a piece of meat to the chow who caught it with practiced ease. "It hardly tastes burned at all."

He'd had enough.

Pushing back from the table, he stood up. "I hate to cut this short, but I have an early flight in the morning."

"Oh, you have to leave so soon? I thought we might play Uno."

"Sorry." He smiled. *Uno? I don't think so.*

Gabrielle followed him to the door. "Tell Temple I said hi."

"I'll do that."

She stood in the doorway waving as he stepped into the elevator.

"Au revoir, monsieur." She blew happy kisses at him.

He'd tell Temple hi, all right, he thought. *Plus a few other things.*

Craig headed straight for the shower when he got home and stood under the hottest water he could take until it ran cool.

His second act was to call Temple.

"I thought we had an agreement." He stretched out on the couch and stared at the ceiling.

"What are you doing home so early?" Temple asked. "It's only nine."

"I held out as long as I could. Did you know Gabrielle is an animal lover?"

He scratched his flat belly. Just thinking about the woman's apartment made him itch.

"Yes, I think she has a cat—"

"Cats. Five. And two dogs."

"Five?"

"Five cats, Temple. And a rottweiler and a chow. Big rottweiler," he clarified. "One with cold eyes that watched me. Big chow. Lots of hair. Shedding. Liked me a whole lot, if you know what I mean."

"I thought she lived in an apartment," Temple said.

"Don't you know where she lives?"

"No. I only see her occasionally. We fly different schedules. You didn't like her?"

"We're not . . . compatible," he said shortly.

"Oh, I thought you would be. I mean, she's fun. A kind of latent flower child. You're so traditional I thought she'd be good for you. Contrast, you know?"

"The woman's apartment is a tinderbox. The cat box stinks so bad it's sickening. I'm not sure, but the methane gas in there could have sent us sky-high. She has five cats, Temple," he repeated. "Five! Plus two dogs. They all sleep in the same room—"

"Oh, Craig—"

"They're big dogs, Temple," he emphasized, more vehemently than before. "Big and amorously aggressive. That damn chow tried to mark me!"

"Did what?" she said, laughing.

"Marked me."

"I'm sorry. I had no idea. Gabby's so relaxed—"

"If she were any more *relaxed* she'd be dead. The dogs would bury her! Nothing gets to her. Cats and dogs all over the place. They eat off her plate, Temple. Her apartment looks like it hasn't been cleaned in a month. Every electrical outlet in the place is overloaded. Her curling iron was burning a hole in the bathroom counter—the woman doesn't own a microwave. She put the ribs, box and all, into the oven to reheat, and set it on fire. This is a woman who's in charge of getting passengers out of a burning plane . . . ?"

"Gabrielle's wonderful at her job," she insisted. "She's virtually unshakable."

He sneezed.

"Are you catching a cold?"

"No, I'm not catching a cold!" He sat up to snag a tissue from a box on the desk. "I'm trying to hack up a fur ball."

"I'm sorry," she said, laughing again. "Next time—"

"Say good night, Temple."

"Uh, good night."

Hanging up, he sneezed again. Next time?
In her dreams.

6

TWO FLIGHTS were running late Monday morning and the terminal was crowded with early-morning commuters and vacationers. The business travelers, still trying to wake up, buried their heads in newspapers. The vacationers, animated by the prospect of their trip, chattered among themselves excitedly.

A sudden hush fell over the two groups and Temple turned to see what was the cause. A man in a pilot's uniform, wearing sunglasses, strolled down the concourse holding onto the harness of a Seeing Eye dog.

"Coming through, coming through."

Temple froze, staring. "Scotty!"

Pushing the sunglasses up on top of his head, Scotty grinned. "Just kidding, folks," he said, sweeping Temple into an impromptu dance step as they continued down the concourse.

"He really is kidding," Temple called back to the stunned crowd.

"Whose dog?"

"A passenger's. Told him I'd take Wolf for a walk."

Craig approached, and the high jinks ceased. Handing the dog over to Pat at the gate, Scotty fell into step with Temple. The three walked toward the turboprop awaiting them.

"Are you trying for the unemployment line?" Craig asked and Scotty chuckled.

"Aw, fliers need a good laugh now and then," Scotty said.

"A blind pilot? When passengers are boarding a plane?"

"Management says to keep 'em laughing."

Temple glanced over her shoulder. "I wonder how many cancellations Alí is fending off right now?" she said, looking in the direction of the ticket counter.

Ascending the steps to the plane, Temple disappeared into the galley, Craig and Scotty into the cockpit. By the time she'd finished double-checking cups, sugar, creamers, and juice, the coffee was ready.

Balancing a tray with two cups, Temple delivered the refreshments to Scotty and Craig who were in the middle of the usual preflight check.

"Coffee?"

"Mmm," Scotty said, a pencil in his mouth, taking his cup.

"Thanks." Craig accepted the cup Temple handed him. "By the way," he said, "here's your checkbook. I finally found that $57.98. Dry cleaning, hair salon and Girl Scout cookies."

Temple winced. "I forgot the cookies!"

"Math never was your strong suit."

He seemed to have gotten over the Gabrielle incident, or at least he wasn't going to mention it.

"The usual payment?" she asked.

"Double chocolate chips this time."

"You'll have them tomorrow morning."

Craig stowed his clipboard, and sat back. "How's the passenger list look?"

"Usual crowd," Temple said. "The ones Scotty didn't scare off with his blind-pilot act." She rapped the copilot on the shoulder.

"Did you get my present?" Craig asked.

"What present?"

He tossed her a package of nuts. Grinning, she caught it, getting the implication immediately. *Nuts to you.*

"I take it you haven't forgotten Gabrielle?"

"I owe you one, Burney."

"I got one already. Thanks, Scotty, for setting me up with Jon."

Scotty wouldn't look up. "Sorry about that, kiddo."

She picked up their empty cups. "And Craig, I'm really am sorry about Gabby. Next time—"

He cut her off. "No next time. You take care of your love life, and I'll take care of mine."

She tossed the package of nuts back at him.

Slipping out of the cabin, she made a mental note to phone Gabrielle the moment she got home and find out her version of the story.

After checking the galley again, Temple took her place at the door of the plane to greet the embarking passengers.

Thirty minutes later, the passengers were safely buckled into their seats and ready for takeoff. A pair of redheaded twins had already alienated everyone within two rows of them. Their mother was showing signs of strain and it wasn't eight-thirty yet.

A bell sounded, and Temple picked up the closed-circuit intercom.

"Ready to fly?" Craig asked.

"Like a bird."

Completing a final walk down the aisle to check seat belts and chair backs, Temple returned to the front, slipped a tape into the cassette player and reached for an oxygen mask as a resonant baritone on the tape relayed vital safety instructions.

Switching off the cassette, Temple smiled and reached for her microphone. Sparrow was known for its good-natured approach to flight information. Sort of sweetening the dry repetitive instructions.

"Good morning, ladies and gentlemen, thank you for flying Sparrow Airlines. We know you had a choice. You will note that in case of the grievous combination of turbulence and weak stomachs, there are bags in the pocket of the seat in front of you. Since I'm the only attendant on board, please use them. And if you must hurl, please hurl accurately."

The twins were hanging over the backs of the seats in front of them, forcing the occupants to lean forward. They were already glancing anxiously over their shoulders. The mother's efforts to reseat the twosome were ineffectual. It was going to be a long flight, Temple decided.

"Should it become necessary to set down this plane in water," she continued, "the cushion of your seat is a flotation device—"

"Water?" someone commented loudly. "When did they put an ocean in Oklahoma?"

"Why should we need flotation devices?" a man in the back row piped up. "I want a parachute."

"In the unlikely event of the sudden loss of cabin pressure, oxygen masks will drop in front of you. Place the bag first on your face, then assist your children—"

The twins found the reading-light switches.

"—if you want to," she added, grinning.

Announcements out of the way, Temple buckled herself into her seat. The plane was barely off the ground before the boys discovered the air flow vents. Temple loaded her refreshment cart with coffee and juice, and began to make her way down the aisle.

It was a typical flight. The twins couldn't decide what to drink, wouldn't sit down, wouldn't leave their trays upright and wouldn't listen to their mother.

Temple finished her run and returned to the cockpit to see if Craig and Scotty needed anything.

Craig glanced up as she came in. "Everything all right back there?"

"Twins from hell in fine form, new mother nicely settled. We've got a male passenger who is taking up two seats and half the aisle, complaining about the no smoking rule in loud tones. Oh, and he thinks he's Casanova. If his knee presses my backside one more time I may do something drastic. In other words, conditions normal."

"There's always one," Scotty commented.

"If we can put a man on the moon, why couldn't we send a select few?" Temple muttered.

"Wouldn't that put a kink in your plans?" Craig mused aloud as he took a gauge reading.

"Maybe I'll just get a cat." After her date with Jon, even a rhino with an infected horn didn't sound bad.

"Ditch the cat idea," Craig intoned.

Scotty graciously changed the subject. "Hey, Craig, Steph has a woman for you—"

Craig threw his hands up in frustration.

"What is it with me? Do I have Idiot stamped across my forehead? Sucker? Fool? Do I look like someone who enjoys pain?"

A buzz interrupted the conversation and Temple voiced a mental "shoot."

"Ten to one it's the knee man."

"I'm betting on the twins." Temple grimaced.

As she left the cabin, Scotty was trying to set Craig up with a woman in Steph's pottery class.

By the time the flight was over, Temple had peeled the twins off the backs of their seats at least three times. She'd also helped the new mother change a soiled diaper in the galley. Diaper service, she decided, was above and beyond the call of duty. By the time they landed in Dallas she was exhausted.

Craig caught up with her as she was leaving the terminal.

She glanced up as he fell into step beside her. How could he fly the hours he did and still look as fresh as the moment he'd arrived in the morning? she wondered. Even a hint of his after-shave remained; Old Spice. She'd read somewhere that in a sniff test recently conducted with a thousand women, they still preferred Old Spice ten to one over other men's after-shave. She'd given Craig a large bottle for Christmas. For a giddy moment, she wondered if he was wearing the tiger-patterned briefs she'd also given him.

Actually, she was far too aware that she was wearing the French-cut scarlet teddy he'd given her.

"Got time for a quick drink?" he asked.

"Sorry, got a date," she said. "And Thia's called twice this week and I haven't returned her call. She'll think I've skipped town."

"We could make it a quick one. You can talk to Thia anytime."

He'd caught her at a weak moment, darn him. An hour with Craig Stevens would make up for the date that Ginny had arranged for her tonight.

"Okay, if it's a quick one."

They cut across the concourse to one of the small airport lounges, and found a table near the back. The waitress took their drink order and disappeared into the shadows.

Craig leaned back and loosened his tie. "You look tired."

"Beautiful but tired," she amended for him. "Why can't men start with the nice before they state the obvious?"

His gaze traveled over her lightly, making her wish she hadn't said anything. "Okay, beautiful but tired. What's wrong?"

Shrugging out of her uniform jacket, she ran her fingers through her hair and massaged her scalp a moment. It felt delicious. "Maybe I'm getting burnout. I'm really beat."

"The knee man?"

"Him, and the twins, and the woman with the fussy baby. I don't know. Maybe it's a good thing I don't have children."

"Marriage, babies, in that order, isn't it?"

"Yeah, so I'm told." She toyed with the candle-holder setting in the middle of the table.

"I think," he said, leaning forward to take her hand, "that you would make a very good mother."

His thumb rubbed across her knuckles, making her heart pound like a trip-hammer.

"Oh, yeah?" Her smile was a little weak. "What makes you think so?"

"Intuition."

"Thought that was a woman thing."

He shrugged, laying her hand carefully back onto the table. "Depends on how well people know each other."

Reaching for her water glass, she wondered if an aspirin would help or hinder at this point. She was so tired her whole body ached.

"Speaking of marriage—"

She looked up. "Were we?"

"I got a wedding invitation from Judi and Rick."

"You've got to be kidding. They've been together—what? Six years?"

"About that," he said.

"One or the other of them has walked out of the relationship at least a dozen times," she said. "What makes them think getting married will change anything?"

Leaning closer, he whispered, "Rumor has it they think they're in love."

"Nuts."

"That's a strange comment coming from someone who's trying her damnedest to find Mr. Right."

"Only because of Grams." She could have bitten her tongue in two.

"Grams?"

"All right, I hate to admit it," she told him, "but I feel kind of obligated to find someone, you know, and settle down, for Grams. She worries about me. Thinks I can't be happy until I'm safely married and have a family of my own. She keeps reminding me how old she is and how she's not going to be around forever—" She stopped speaking and drew a weary breath.

She hadn't meant to tell him why she'd embarked on this plan to find a suitable mate, but now that it was in the open she was relieved. At least he would know why she'd been dating so much lately.

He frowned slightly. "That's what this is all about? This sudden dating frenzy? To please your grandmother?"

The waitress returned with their drinks. Temple extracted the straw from her glass and took a quick sip to give herself a moment to think. She and Craig were close, told each other nearly everything, but not *everything*.

"Of course it isn't *just* to please Grams." She toyed with her glass. There was such a thing as being too close. "I'm thirty-one. Time is slipping away. I like my job, like my apartment, but . . . well, I want to be young enough to enjoy my children—''

"Ticktock, ticktock."

"No," she said, trying to lighten the atmosphere a little. "I'm not in a panic about my biological clock, but right about now I feel a bit run-down."

He smiled warmly, and she relaxed. Discussing marriage always made her tense. Craig too. Maybe she wasn't as ready to settle down as she'd thought.

"So, who's the man of choice tonight?"

"Oh, someone Ginny's significant other knows from work."

"You don't sound enthused," he said. "Don't trust Mike's taste in men?"

"With the luck I'm having lately, I don't trust my own taste in men."

"Or women," he added, sipping his drink.

Her gaze softened. "I really am sorry about Gabrielle. When we were in flight school, she was perfectly normal. Fun, a little crazy sometimes, but definitely not eccentric."

"Nuts," he clarified.

"Eccentric."

"Okay, eccentrically nuts."

Agreeing to disagree, they lifted their glasses in a salute and drank to the compromise.

Craig's gaze lingered on her. "While we're on the subject, I have someone I want you to meet."

Temple bit into a slice of lime, studying him warily. After the Gabrielle incident, she wasn't certain a bit of revenge wasn't behind his suggestion.

"I don't know, Craig—"

"Isn't that the agreement?" he said, arching his eyebrows. "You set me up with your friends, I set you up with mine?"

"Okay," she relented. "Who is it?"

"Dwight Mason."

She frowned. "Have I ever met him?"

"No, but you'll like him." He finished his drink.

"What's he do?"

"Makes money. Lots of it. He's an entrepreneur of sorts."

"Of sorts? I don't know—"

"Sure you do. That's the agreement. I'll call and set it up. Early next week okay with you?"

A deal was a deal. There was no way out. She sincerely wished that she'd never thought up this stupid arrangement. She didn't want Craig mad at her when it didn't work out. Case in point—Gabrielle.

Finishing her drink, she managed a smile. "I'm free any night except Tuesday."

"Good. I'll call Dwight."

They left the lounge together. When they reached their cars, Temple had to squeeze into the driver's side of her pickup. Craig had won the race for the parking space that morning.

"Oh, by the way," he said. "Don't wear the red dress when you go out with Dwight."

"Which red dress?"

He shut her door and she rolled down the window. "The one that fits you like a second skin."

That was strange. It sounded as if he didn't like that dress. She'd paid a week's salary for it and worn the garment to the airline's annual Christmas party last year. He had demanded nearly every dance and they'd had a great time.

"Why not?"

"Dwight doesn't like red," was his dry comment. "Have a good time."

His hands slapped the windowsill as she started the engine.

"Craig," she said, studying his face, "why do I have the distinct impression you're setting me up?"

"I am setting you up."

"No, I mean, 'setting me up,'" she said with emphasis. "Remember the agreement? We don't arrange dates with people we wouldn't go with ourselves. A blind date isn't really a blind date this way. I thought Gabrielle—"

"Relax." He smiled, bending to look in the window. "I've recovered from that overdose of fur. Of course, I may have a feline phobia for the rest of my life," he said. "And have a good time tonight. By the way, what's your date tonight do?"

"He's an accountant. Steady, logical. Dull, but after some of the dates I've had lately, dull is good. Sounds promising. What about you? Got a date tonight?"

"Mmm. An antique-store owner."

"Antiques? Old books and distressed wood? Should be interesting. Bill set you up?"

"No, Dave tricked . . . uh, convinced me to see this one," he told her. "She's twenty-eight, blond, green-eyed and teaches a class on authentication. I asked her about that blue vase—it's good, by the way."

"It ought to be. I bought it for you."

"I know."

His gaze met hers. No one had eyes as blue as his; eyes that could dance with humor or flash with anger. Right now, she wasn't sure what was behind the intensity in his gaze but her heart did that funny little skip-beat that made her forget to breathe.

"I found it in a little dusty shop in Balboa," she said, trying to keep her voice steady. "I don't think the owner knew it was real, but I did."

"Well, Angela says it's a nice piece. You have good taste."

"At least in antiques. You sure you're not setting me up with this Dwight to get even with me?"

"You're getting paranoid, Burney."

"Like I don't have a reason?"

He smiled. "Would I do that to you?"

"Yeah. You would." She laughed, feeling better.

As she drove away, Temple glanced in the rearview mirror, watching Craig get into the Lincoln.

This Dwight better be good, or I'll dig up another Gabrielle. This time on purpose.

After a hot shower, Temple stretched out on the bed to pen her weekly letter to Grams. She paused for a moment, mentally sorting through her recent dates in an attempt to put her reactions to them into words. They were too dismal to report. Instead, she found her thoughts drifting to Craig.

No, she told herself, firmly.

Dear Grams,

Have I told you about my good friend, Craig Stevens—

What is it with you today, Burney? He puts his hand on your shoulder to slide past you and you get as giddy as a teenager. Then you dissect every tone of voice and every nuance of speech. Maybe this "dating game" she'd embarked on was getting to her. She quit chewing the top of her pen and continued her letter.

He's handsome, smart, witty and one of the best pilots Sparrow employs. Helen and Frank should be proud of him—you tell them so when you see them in church Sunday.

I guess what I'm trying to say is that's the problem, Grams. But our friendship is just too good to jeopardize it by dating each other. Besides, he's a pilot. And that's enough said about that.

She stopped writing as she considered what she'd just told Grams. It would hurt to lose him, she admitted to herself. Hurt too much. Besides, with Nancy still caring about Craig, obviously still hoping something would work out, anything more than friendship between them would complicate things too much. She couldn't bear it if something happened to destroy the special relationship she and Craig had. If...if he decided to sever their friendship, it would kill her. She fully understood how Nancy felt. Losing Craig would be far too painful. She resumed her letter.

Hope everything is well with you. I will make it home for Christmas. Hang the tinsel and stuff the goose.

Love,
Tootie

P.S. You'll be glad to know I'm dating on a regular basis. Can't say I'm having any success, but I am going out.

Sealing the letter, she rolled off the bed.

Oh, yes, Grams. I'm going out, for all the good it's doing me. So far, I'm zero for fourteen, but who's counting?

7

REJECTING FIRST a long skirt and Victorian-style blouse, then rose slacks and matching sweater, then tan slacks and chocolate-colored long shirt, and a black tube dress she considered too adventurous for a first date, Temple finally settled on a two-piece turquoise casual suit.

It's nerves, Burney. Plain ole nerves. After the last few dates she'd suffered through, she was paranoid, that was all. It wasn't logical that her string of disastrous dates could continue. Even a blind squirrel found a nut every once in a while, so the odds that tonight should be a winner were running high.

Still, she vacillated between calling Bill Moffit and making up some excuse as to why she couldn't go out tonight, and hoping he'd call and break the date himself.

Neither happened.

Standing in front of an antique mirror in the foyer, she was trying to decide whether to rebrush her hair so it waved away from her face, when the doorbell sounded.

"Darn," she whispered. "Darn, darn, darn."

Forcing a smile, she went to the door. Somehow, she kept the smile steady when she found herself face-to-face with a man no taller than herself.

Okay, this is okay. Height is no problem. Only a person with a small mind worries about height.

He was wearing a three-piece charcoal suit, white shirt, gray and white paisley tie with a diamond tack. She relaxed a little. At least he wasn't wearing a straw hat with a pineapple stuck in it.

"Bill?"

"Temple?" He extended his hand. "Bill Moffit."

He didn't yell, or mumble. "Hello, Bill. Would you like a drink before we go?"

"No." He glanced at his watch and at that moment it chimed. "I made reservations at Antonio's."

"Oh . . . well, I'm ready. Let me get my jacket."

Antonio's. Five-star restaurant. Maybe I should have worn something a little more formal.

Bill's car was an older-model charcoal BMW with leather interior. It smelled like old paper.

"What kind of music do you like?" he asked as they got in. "I've got anything you want."

Reaching into the back seat, he flipped open a leather case that held at least a hundred eight-tracks. Eight-tracks! Temple mentally groaned.

"Um, country?"

He looked at her as if she'd lost her mind.

"That isn't even a choice," he said. "Try R&B, show tunes, opera, Barbra Streisand. She's in a class by herself."

"Barbra's fine."

After fiddling with the dinosaurian eight-track player to get what he considered the "exact" right setting, Bill finally started the car and merged with the traffic. Driving with one hand on the wheel, the other draped loosely over the back of her seat, he hummed along with the music.

This is fine. I'm having a whiteout as far as small talk is concerned, but that's okay. Small talk is overrated anyway.

Antonio's was a pricey restaurant specializing in authentic Italian cuisine. The mouth-watering aromas of garlic and pasta drifted into the foyer as they worked their way up to the host.

"Table for Moffit," Bill said.

"Yes, sir. It will be just a moment, sir."

He looked at Temple, smiling. "Ten minutes. Tops."

"No problem," Temple said, watching a teenager feed dough into a pasta machine then catch the noodles it produced. Somehow, the limp pasta reminded her of her love life. Colorless, flavorless, no body.

The waiting area was too crowded for them to engage in conversation. As they were gradually shoved against one wall, Bill jingled change in his pocket impatiently. The room grew close and the aromas of garlic and tomato sauce were getting to her. A small headache was forming at the nape of her neck. Temple wished she'd followed her first instinct and called off the date. But if she had, she told herself, Ginny would never have let her forget it.

"Moffit, party of two?"

"That's us," Bill said, his hand firmly clasping her elbow to direct her to follow the hostess.

They followed the woman to a corner booth that, if Temple had wanted to consider it as such, could be called romantic. The restaurant's cozy, dark corners, candles on the tables, soft music, the low tones of conversation, made her relax just a little.

A waiter in a modified black tux approached to take their drink order.

"No drinks," Bill said quickly, then glanced at her as if he'd just remembered she was there. "Okay?"

"Fine."

The waiter smiled. "Then permit me to tell you tonight's specials."

"Shoot," Bill said.

They listened as he recited the list.

"Thanks," Bill said when the man had finished. "We'll need a few minutes to look over the menu."

"And what will you be drinking with your dinner, sir?"

"Iced tea is $1.50," Bill mumbled. His forehead furrowed in thought as his gaze skimmed the menu choices.

"Sir?"

"Iced tea. Iced tea."

"Thank you. Madam?"

Temple followed Bill's lead. "Tea with lemon, please."

Bill was still studying the menu when the waiter left. He let out a low whistle. "It's been a while since I've been here," he said. "They've upped the prices."

"They are a little high—"

"Never mind. Order what you want. What looks good?"

"Well, the manicotti sounds good."

He whistled again. "At $18.95 it should be."

Made uneasy by his tone, Temple quickly rechecked the columns. "Well, there's always lasagna."

Bill started figuring on a napkin, shaking his head. The waiter appeared beside him, order pad at the ready.

"What may I get for you tonight?"

"Temple?"

Swallowing, Temple's gaze swept down the menu, checking the midpriced items.

Apparently the cost of the entrées is going to be a problem for Bill. So why did he bring me to a five-star restaurant? Great thinking.

She closed the menu. "Pasta fagiole with a salad." *Soup and salad. You can't get much cheaper than that, Burney.*

"Excellent. And you, sir?"

"I'll have the…spaghetti, no meat sauce. Does that come in a luncheon portion?"

"No sir, not for the dinner meal."

"Okay. Spaghetti."

"Salad, sir?"

"No salad. Does the bread come with the entrée? Or is it charged separately?"

The waiter seemed surprised by the question. "Uh, why it comes as a courtesy, sir."

"At these prices, I'd hope so." He handed both menus to him. "Hustle a basket out here."

After a brief hesitation, the waiter spun on his heel and left, a pained look on his face.

"Now then," Bill said, settling his elbows on the table, holding up his tea glass to inspect it for smudges, "tell me about yourself."

"I'm a flight attendant. I fly with Sparrow Airlines."

"How long have you been flying?"

"Ten years. Five years with Sparrow."

"Have you ever thought about doing anything else? I mean, can you be a hostess until you retire?"

"Well, I never thought about it," Temple admitted. "The airlines have less strict guidelines now than a few years ago so I guess I could fly as long as I want to."

A devilish look came into his eyes. "How old are you?"

She glanced up, surprised.

"Only kidding," he said. "I don't expect you to admit your age." Setting down his glass, he leaned forward. "You women have to stay pretty thin. How much do you weigh?"

Damn! Another one bites the dust.

Over dinner, Bill dominated the conversation. Temple ate, listening with one ear as her mind raced with reasons she shouldn't leave right then. Rude, she decided. No use wasting good food.

"Well, you'll be settling down with a family soon," he was saying. "Statistics show that a woman is usually married by the time she's twenty-three. That's up two years from ten years ago. A man is normally twenty-five, up three years. Though women usually work until they're twenty-eight before having children. Still, most continue to work after the kids come along. Economics being what they are today, the woman is taken out of the home to work as well as raise the children.

"They shouldn't, though. Too much stress in trying to work and keep house, especially when there are children."

An alarm bell went off in her head. "Men don't help raise the children?"

"Not at first. Women are better nurturers," he proclaimed. "Statistics tell us that men are assuming more of a role with younger children, but I'm not sure those figures aren't skewed by men wanting to take advantage of the family-leave opportunity afforded them now. Women, you have to admit, are better with children. How about you? Planning to have children?"

"Not right away." Like Craig said, marriage first and that prospect was looking dimmer by the moment.

"Can't wait too long. You're over thirty."

She didn't like the turn of this conversation at all. "I understand you're a CPA, Bill?"

"Yes. With Whitney, Mannes, Gowan and Peterson. One day, Moffit will be added to that door. Within five years is my plan."

Accounting? Good ole Bill here could balance her checkbook and do her taxes for her.

"Do you have an area of specialty?"

"Corporate taxes. Though I really enjoy the statistical format." He leaned back with obvious satisfaction. "At the moment, I'm deep into a complicated audit. A utility company. I suspect they're not using their invested funds properly and I know they're not reporting income from those investments. You wouldn't believe what people think they can get away with . . . or at least fail to find out that they've got to report. And these people are supposed to be trained and informed."

"Must be complicated," Temple murmured, her eyes starting to glaze over. An image of him naked surrounded by ledger books flashed in her mind, and she recoiled.

"It is. I've been working on this one area for a week now and I've just begun to scratch the surface. By the time I'm finished," he said pompously, "they're going to have quite an education in how to use a reporting system—"

He droned on, detailing the steps he was taking to track down errors in the company's accounting system, none of which she understood. Math had never been her strong point—witness her inability to balance her checkbook. Craig kept telling her it was simple. Mark off the checks returned with the bank statement with a red pen along with noted deposits, add up those not checked off—and she lost him there. Though she followed instructions carefully, somehow her checkbook never balanced out.

But then, Craig made everything look easy.

Bill never missed a beat in his continuing narrative about various complicated tax situations he'd had to unravel over the past two years. It seemed that most of them required several weeks of intense work equal to the development of the atomic bomb—work he was obviously willing to relate in intricate detail. But, he'd said not once but three times, it was soooo satisfying when the last column of figures was added up and balanced, stacks of forms completed perfectly and presented to the errant comptroller or head accountant.

"May I offer you one of our wonderful desserts," the waiter suggested, displaying a tray of luscious-looking plaster facsimiles. "Spumoni, of course, French silk pie and a light pastry—"

"Nothing for me. Temple?" Bill was figuring on the napkin again.

Temple eyed the French silk, but knew she didn't dare order. Bill was already calculating the total of their meal and frowning.

"No, thanks. Maybe coffee, though."

"We have a very nice latte, or perhaps a cappuccino?"

"Latte, please," Temple ordered. To heck with Bill. He'd chosen the place. He should have checked out the prices first if that was a concern.

"And you, sir?"

"Just decaf."

"Cream, sir? There's no extra charge."

"No, black."

The waiter's remark went right past Bill and Temple swallowed a laugh.

The latte was exquisite. Temple leisurely sipped it as Bill continued his litany of tax errors most common to companies as compared to individual tax problems. Her mind began to numb.

How was it possible, she wondered, to sit through an entire evening and not understand a single word the man said? How was it possible for an evening with such bright promise to dim so completely?

"They hadn't even filed—"

The waiter discreetly slipped the bill onto the table. "Thank you for dining with us this evening. I'll take care of this for you whenever you're ready."

As soon as he'd left, Bill picked up the bill. His hair stood on end. "Forty-one eighty? How is that possible?" He began frantically retotaling his columns. "Mine was $18.85, yours . . . $10.50. How much was the latte? More than the decaf? Decaf $.95. Latte?"

"Two seventy-five, I think. Look, if there's a problem, I've got—"

"This bill can't be right. Forty-one? Waiter? Will you come here, please?"

Temple shifted slightly in the booth, hoping to lose herself in the deeper shadows. If he was going to quibble about cost, she wished he would at least lower his voice. The occupants of three tables around them had heard him and made their annoyance clear. Painful memories of the Darrell fiasco surfaced.

The waiter whipped to a stop at the table, bending slightly at the waist with a look of genuine concern in his expression. "Is there a problem, sir?"

"This bill is not right. Forty-one eighty for what we had? And that doesn't include tax and tip? Highway robbery!!"

"Sir, I'm sure there's been no mistake, but I can have the cashier recheck it for you—"

"I've checked it. I'm only questioning the prices. Who sets these prices? Donald Trump?"

"I'll call the manager, sir."

"Bill," Temple said, leaning forward and lowering her voice. "If there's a problem—"

"Nothing that can't be taken care of. These places try slipping a couple dollars here, a couple dollars there. Just in case someone doesn't tip. You know how it is."

Temple felt her face grow warm as more people glanced in their direction, whispering among themselves.

The manager appeared. "Is there a problem, sir?"

"Your prices are too high!" Bill re-added and came up with the same total.

Frowning, he crossed off the total and re-added the bill again. "Well, I guess it's right—highway robbery, but right." He handed the ticket back to the waiter.

"Would you bring me a to-go container for this? Waste not want not, that's my motto," he said sanctimoniously.

"Are the refills on coffee free? My cup's empty. You're slipping."

Temple had to give the waiter top marks for holding on to his temper when he most likely wanted to shoot Bill. She knew she did.

"And you, madam? May I freshen your latte?" the man asked politely.

Quickly, shielding the cup with her hand, she shook her head. "No!"

"More bread, Temple? It's free."

"No, thank you."

"I'll need a receipt, too," Bill added, flashing his Gold Card.

The waiter slipped away with the credit card as Bill carefully counted out six one-dollar bills and some change. He placed them squarely in the middle of the table with a little satisfied pat of his fingertips.

"How long have you known Mike and Ginny?" Temple asked, curious as to how the three had gotten together, especially since Ginny didn't have a thrifty bone in her body.

"Only on a professional basis," he told her. "I did their taxes several years ago. I know everything about their financial situation, but other than that we seldom see one another. Seem like nice folks, though. They've referred several clients to me. I appreciate a prudent person."

No kidding. I'd appreciate having a smooth exit line.

"Ah, here we are," Bill crowed when the waiter returned.

He quickly signed the credit card form, carefully tore out the carbons and folded them, then slipped them into his pocket along with his receipt. When another couple left the table across the aisle without taking their receipt, Bill reached over and took it, too—for his records.

"You can never be too careful," he said. "One of my clients got his credit card statement and someone had run up a thousand dollars on his bill. Fortunately, he was able to get the charges removed. You have to be on your toes. Lots of crooks out there. Ready to go?"

She had been ready an hour ago.

More Streisand on the way home. If she heard "People Who Need People" one more time, she'd slap Bill just for the satisfaction of it.

He parked the BMW in front of her apartment building and turned toward her.

"I had a good time this evening. May I call you again?"

This was it; bailout time. "I'm never sure what my schedule will be."

"No problem. I'll check with Ginny."

She slipped out of the car before he could say anything more, and shut the door. Giving a brief wave, she ran up the stairs and into her apartment.

Switching on a lamp, she stood a moment to enjoy the soft light bathing the small but cozy room in a warm, welcoming glow. Home sweet home. Her headache began slipping away and she drew a deep, cleansing breath to calm her nerves.

She dropped her purse onto the couch, kicked off her shoes and continued into the kitchen to pour herself a glass of milk.

Leaning against the cabinet, Temple stared out the window. Mrs. King's lights were off. She went to bed with the birds. One by one, the lights on the block went off as people turned off televisions, put the cat out, and pulled the shades.

She sighed as she thought of the five years she'd spent in the crowded but energetic Dallas/Fort Worth area. There was something here for everyone. The problem was, what was that something for her?

Lately, her life reminded her of the old story about the planeload of passengers who were waiting for drinks to be served, when they spotted their flight attendant crawling down the aisle, frantically peering under seats and around feet. Amazed, they watched as she leaped up and continued her frenzied search through the upper storage compartments.

"What's going on?" one passenger finally demanded.

The harried attendant whirled. "I'm looking for the romance that was promised me!"

The untutored believed the stories about hostesses meeting and marrying first-class megabucks men. The tantalizing tales of lengthy layovers in exotic locales. The crew parties with cases of French champagne.

Temple had never really expected romance. Hoped for it, maybe. The travel was still a nice part of her job. But she'd dreamed that among the new people she met there would have been someone special.

Temple sighed again, drinking her milk as she gazed at the night sky.

Bright stars dotted the velvet-black sky, and the sliver of a moon hung over the backyard fence. A perfect night, if only there was the perfect man to spend it with.

Drawing a deep breath, she padded into the living room and relaxed on the couch, flexing her toes as she closed her eyes.

Who was the perfect man?

Not Bill Moffit.

Nor the pet store owner who had a passion for boas and thought she should have one of his slithering friends as a roommate.

Nor the car salesman who had the perfect deal for her; the advertising copywriter who'd been all puffed up with pride because he'd been nominated for a local ADDY award; nor the television cameraman who was impressed by his acquaintance with a minor celebrity who hosted an area talk show; nor the minor league baseball player whose total focus was on getting to "the bigs." Not a "perfect" man among them. Forget perfection. She'd settle for normal.

A man who could carry on a normal conversation, not a running narrative.

A man who was sensitive, concerned, interested in something other than himself and his own small world.

She carried her milk into the bathroom and stared at her reflection in the mirror over the sink.

Where was the man who could appreciate who she was and what she wanted to do? A man who made a woman feel strong and confident, yet protected and needed.

Her mouth turned down as she remembered the evening she'd just survived.

A man who didn't total his date's dinner on a napkin.

A man like Craig.

Nuts.

8

"STEVENS AN airline pilot. Who would've thought it?" Jack Ladue leaned forward, a knowing grin in his eyes. "What's the attraction? The flight attendants? Eh?" Jabbing Craig in the ribs, he grinned. "What I wouldn't give to be in your shoes."

Craig smiled. He and Jack had been passing friends in college, but they hadn't kept in touch except to exchange the occasional Christmas card. When Jack had called to say he was in town, they'd made plans to meet.

"Wow, who's the fox?" Jack murmured as he spotted Temple coming through the lounge door.

Craig followed Jack's gaze and saw she was accompanied by a tall, dark-haired man tonight. She was laughing up at him, and he was responding with a quick squeeze of her shoulders.

"She's a flight attendant with Sparrow."

"Whoooe. Redheads. Don't you love 'em," Jack drawled, dramatically emphasizing the accent he'd picked up from his years in Oklahoma as a representative with an oil company. "What's her name, and what's her number?"

"Sorry, she's off-limits." At least to men like Jack.

"You dating her?"

"Just friends."

"Then why the objection?" Jack swiveled back to look at Craig. "I want her."

Craig watched as Temple and her date were seated.

"Introduce me," Jack said. "I'm a good catch. Single, employed, all-around American guy."

Craig pointedly looked at his watch and stood. "Sorry to cut this short, Jack, but I've got some things to do at the airport."

Clearly oblivious to Craig's cool tone, Jack stood and stuck out his hand. "Good to see you again, buddy." His gaze went back to Temple's table. "I think I'll just stay here and girl-watch for a while. Give you a call next time I'm in town."

"Sounds good." Craig glanced in Temple's direction, frowning when her date leaned closer and laughed at something she said.

She looked good tonight, damn good. Her new haircut framed her face, giving her a perky kind of Kathy Lee Gifford look that made heads turn. Who was the man? No one he knew. For a moment, he entertained the idea of going over to introduce himself on the pretext of business, but he decided against it. With another glance over his shoulder, Craig quickly strode out of the lounge.

He spent the evening prowling his apartment trying to find something to occupy his mind. Three times he picked up the phone. Twice he even dialed Temple's number. He thought about leaving a message, but couldn't think of anything to say.

What was the matter with him? He'd picked out dates for Temple. Why should it bother him that she was out with somebody she'd chosen herself?

He didn't know why, exactly, but it did.

SATURDAY MORNING, Temple spotted Craig's Lincoln approaching the airport gate. Punching the accelerator, she sent her truck spurting forward and grinned when his Lincoln followed a millisecond later.

She had a bone to pick with him. Dwight Mason had turned out to be nice. A definite improvement over the men Temple had dated lately. Dwight was kind, courteous, successful, attentive, generous—but dull as a box of rocks. Craig couldn't spot a loser any better than her other friends.

Cutting off the Lincoln, she whipped into her parking spot, slammed on the brakes and killed the engine. Once again the Silverado blocked two spaces in her best lane-sharking style.

The Lincoln's brakes squawked, then Craig slowly backed it up. After several tries, he managed to squeeze the car into the space left between Temple's truck and Ginny's small Ford.

Sliding out of her pickup, Temple wiggled her fingers at him. "Captain Stevens."

Craig maneuvered his shoulders out of his car, and nearly fell onto the asphalt as he tried to stand. Temple bit back a grin.

"Burney, one of these days—"

"Threats don't faze me, Stevens. By the way, Dwight was nice, but we didn't hit it off."

"Oh?"

"Nope. Sorry."

He handed her a large manila envelope, and fell into step beside her. "Here are your tax forms. I had to leave out a couple of good deductions because you didn't have receipts. Other than that, you're in good shape."

She slid a sly look his direction, her eyebrows arching.

"Your tax form, Burney. Get your mind out of the gutter."

Grinning, Temple matched his stride. Threatening clouds hung overhead promising rain any moment. She hoped the flight wasn't bumpy. All she needed today was a full plane of airsick commuters.

"Guess I should take a leaf from Bill's book," she said.

"Bill?"

"Wednesday night's date."

"You mean last night."

She glanced at him. "No, Wednesday night. Your dud, Dwight Mason, Monday, Keith Wilson, Tuesday, Bill Moffit—"

"Who were you with last night?"

Was that an attitude in his voice? "That was you!" She punched his arm lightly. "I thought I recognized your back going out the front door last night." She'd recognize his backside in a cast of five hundred, but she wasn't about to tell him that. "Why didn't you say hello?"

"You looked busy."

There was that tone again. "Not really."

"Who was the guy?"

"Kirk Petersen."

"Little young for you, isn't he?"

"Twenty-two? I'm not that ancient, am I?"

"Who is this jock?"

"He goes to my gym. We stopped for a drink after we worked out—but back to Wednesday night's date. Craig, you wouldn't believe this one."

"Oh, I probably will."

"You'd like him, though. He's got this receipt thing down to a science. He's a CPA."

"Did you have a good time?"

What *was* that tone? Jealousy? Nah. It couldn't be—not Craig.

"Bombastic. I love going out with guys who quibble over the cost of entrées in a five-star restaurant. Quibble loudly."

He grinned.

"Kill the grin. He added the check over and over on a napkin. Wait until Ginny tries to set me up again."

"Maybe she thought he'd be good for you. You could use a lesson or two in economics."

"Why? I have you," she said dryly. "Besides, Dwight wasn't exactly a barrel of laughs, either. I had to poke him to make sure he was still alive."

"No go, huh?"

"I thought he might be mechanical and someone forgot to wind him up. Talk about your deadpan face."

"Well, he does tend to clam up when he's nervous."

They turned toward the terminal.

"Well, scratch him off your list," she said. "Did you ever call Miranda?"

"Called her. Shouldn't have. What is this thing you have about blondes? Have I ever given you the impression I enjoy a woman who speaks in one-syllable words?"

"Sorry. Mandy's cute. The cheerleader type. I thought you'd make a nice couple."

"Think substance, Burney. Women who have something between the ears. I like conversation with breakfast."

"Oh." She glanced up at him. "Got to breakfast, did you?"

There it was again. That little stab of something she hated to call jealousy. But the idea of Craig with a woman was more than she wanted to consider—and that was crazy, especially since she was the one who'd set up this mutual-dating plan in the first place.

Craig stopped in front of Temple, forcing her to stop also. "What?" she said.

"I don't go to bed with every woman I meet."

"I—" She felt a little foolish. "It was only a comment."

His gaze met hers intently as if he was measuring her response.

"I know you don't sleep around. What's the problem?"

Craig shook his head. "I don't know. I just... this dating thing is getting to me."

"I know the feeling."

They stood for a moment as if there was something more to say.

But when neither came up with it, Craig reached for the door of the terminal building and held it open. "After you."

Inside the terminal, Craig waved at Flo behind the car rental counter as he headed toward the pilots' lounge. Temple walked over to the lunch counter. Ginny was busy taking an order from an elderly couple, so Temple poured herself a cup of coffee and waited for her friend to finish.

"Hi," Ginny said, taking two sweet rolls out of the case and sliding them into the microwave. "What's up?"

"Not much." Swiveling on the stool, Temple turned to look at Craig's retreating back. "Maybe my temperature, a little."

"Anything to do with the hunk over there? Saw you walk in with Craig."

"Yeah."

"Any man who looks like that is too good to waste on just friendship. Don't you ever wonder what he's like?"

"I don't have to wonder, I know what he's like." That was the problem. She was starting to compare every man she met to Craig. The others came up short—way short.

Ginny laughed.

"What, what?" Temple said, tossing the last of her coffee into the sink.

"Admit it, you're attracted to him. And not just as a buddy."

"Buddies don't mess up good friendships by dating each other."

Ginny rinsed cups and set them in a drain rack before putting them into the dishwasher.

"You're missing a good thing," she said. "He's gorgeous. Every flight attendant I know recognizes that— married *and* single."

"Even you?"

"Especially me."

"Get a grip, Gin." Temple picked up her bag, uneasy with the subject of Craig. She left with a good-natured wave, and started down the concourse to check in.

As she approached the bottom steps into the plane, Scotty came into view. The surprised look on the faces of nearby passengers made Temple take a closer look.

Scotty had a large book tucked beneath his arm.

"Good morning, Flight Attendant Burney. Fine morning it is."

Temple got a look at the book—*How to Fly the Saab*.

Trying to keep a straight face, she mounted the stairs. Scotty followed, strutting through the cabin with the fake book innocently tucked beneath his arm. The few early boarders strained to read the title, chuckling at one another when they did.

Inside the galley, Temple checked supplies and then started the coffee.

Thirty minutes later, all passengers were boarded. When everyone was settled with seat belts in place, Scotty made another walk-through, the book still tucked beneath his arm.

"Good morning, good morning," he greeted as he walked up and down the aisle.

Returning to the cockpit, he slid the door open and inquired in a loud voice, "Captain Stevens, boy am I glad you showed up. Do you remember how to fly this thing? I didn't get past chapter five in the book last night."

The open laughter assured Temple that the passengers understood their copilot was a buffoon.

One day, someone is going to fall for his routine and I'm going to let him do the explaining.

Temple braced herself against the forward bulkhead, microphone in hand, preparing to make the usual announcements. With the mood set for the flight, she took advantage of the affable atmosphere.

"Ladies and gentlemen, we'd like to apologize for the delay in leaving the gate this morning. The machine that usually smashes your luggage is broken so the ground crew is having to crush it by hand."

More giggles.

She continued the patter for a few minutes then, announcements finished, Temple was returning to the galley when a hand reached out and caught her arm.

"How about half a cup of coffee, honey, little cream, sprinkle of sugar."

"Good morning, Mr. Carlson. This isn't your usual flight. Special sales meeting?"

"Convention. High times this weekend." He grinned widely. "Just barely got a hotel reservation."

"Well, I hope you have a good time—"

"I'd have a better time if you'd go to tonight's banquet with me."

"Mr. Carlson—"

"I know, no fraternizing with the passengers. Can't blame a guy for tryin'." He grinned again, his teeth like piano keys in his puffy face.

And trying and trying and trying, she thought, still smiling.

She continued toward the galley, taking orders for drinks as she went. An hour later, she had spoken with each passenger, delivered beverages, answered a half-dozen questions about connecting flights and cleaned up one spilled orange juice.

As the plane began to descend into Houston, Temple finished gathering up used cups, making sure seat belts were in place and trays and backs upright. An approaching weather front had made the flight unpleasant this morning. They had flown through fog for the past thirty minutes.

Scotty was at the controls. He was an excellent pilot, but his landings were never as smooth as Craig's. Wind gusts this morning made the landing bumpier than usual. The plane sat down hard, bounced, then landed again.

Temple smiled at the anxious looks out the window.

Once down, the plane taxied smoothly to the terminal. Temple picked up the hand mike again.

"Thank you for flying with us today," she said. "If you enjoyed your flight, remember it was American Sparrow 2632." She winked. "If you didn't, then it was American Eagle 3216."

Even nervous passengers managed a laugh as they began gathering their belongings. Temple took her place at the door, smiling as the passengers deplaned.

By the time Temple finished cleaning up the galley and clearing the cabin, it was nearly noon. Scotty and Craig finished about the same time and exited with her.

The drizzle grew heavier as the three hurried across the tarmac. Scotty frowned at the darkening sky. "I'd say we're going to be stuck here for a while."

Temple glanced up, assessing the rapidly worsening weather. "What did the tower say?"

"Heavy fog," Craig and Scotty concurred simultaneously.

Scotty went ahead to check on the conditions for their return flight.

"It's like we thought," he said when he met them in the staff lounge later.

Temple had kicked off her shoes and sat with her feet tucked beneath her. Craig had shoved his tie into his pocket as soon as they'd entered the staff area, tossed his jacket across the back of a chair and unbuttoned his collar. He was the sort of man who looked great in a uniform, and even better dressed casually. He'd run his fingers through his hair, letting it curl over his forehead. The afternoon shadow of a beard made his rugged good looks even more profound.

"How bad?" Temple asked, dragging her attention from Craig's profile.

"Another ten minutes and we're socked in. No flights in or out of Houston until the fog lets up, which the weather bureau advises will be around midmorning tomorrow, earliest."

"Well, that does it." Craig stood and stretched. "Let's get a hotel room."

"If we can find any. Mr. Carlson said there are several conventions in town," Temple said, picking up the empty soft-drink cups and dumping them into the trash can.

Craig tucked a phone receiver under his chin and punched in a number. Temple gathered up her things and shoved her feet back into her shoes.

"Nothing?" he said.

Temple heard him and paused.

"Any suggestions?" he said and disconnected the call.

"Ramada?" she guessed.

Craig punched another number.

"Yes, a single, or anything you've got."

His gaze met hers and he shook his head.

"Thanks."

Another number, and the same response.

Hanging up the phone, Craig looked grim. "Between the conventions and fog, looks like we're stuck in the employees' lounge."

"Not me," Scotty said. "I've got a cousin lives here. I'm giving him a call. He's in an efficiency or I'd—"

"Thanks," Craig said.

Giving them an apologetic wave, Scotty left.

"Well, what now?" she asked.

Craig picked up the phone and dialed again. When the other end answered, he inquired about a room.

"Hold on." He held the receiver to his shoulder. "They've got one room. It's a dump, but it's better than sleeping in the lounge. Do you want it?"

"Only one room?"

"You better grab it."

"That would mean you're stuck on the couch here. I'd feel guilty."

"We need to decide. Wait, I'll flip you for it." He dug into his pocket for a coin and came up with a quarter. "Heads or tails."

"Heads."

He flipped the coin, catching it deftly. "Heads. You win." He put the receiver to his ear. She could have sworn the coin had landed tails up in his hand.

"Wait," she said.

Craig let the receiver slide, arching his eyebrows inquiringly.

She shrugged. "We can share. I hate to think of you sleeping on one of these couches."

Craig eyed the narrow sofa. A vinyl and chrome torture rack.

"You're sure?"

"Hey, I trust you," she said. They were friends. He could take the sofa at the hotel.

Craig hesitated a moment, then spoke into the phone, his gaze locked with hers.

"I'll take it. Craig Stevens. Yes. It might take us thirty minutes or so to get there." He gave them his credit card number and dropped the receiver back into the cradle.

"Okay. We've got a room."

"Uh-huh," she picked up her purse, feeling suddenly awkward. She wished she wasn't quite so conscious of him. "We'd better claim it before they double the rate and give it to someone else."

The fog was as thick as pea soup. They waited for more than thirty minutes before a cab edged to the curb in front of the terminal. The driver rolled down the window and leaned out. "Can't see your hand in front of your face, but if you're not going far I'll give it a try."

"Just a couple of miles." Craig gave him the name of the hotel, and opened the back door for Temple.

"Luggage?" the cabbie asked.

"No luggage."

The driver grinned as they crawled into the back seat.

"What about pajamas?" Temple asked.

His eyes locked lazily with hers. "What about them?"

Temple's pulse leaped at the innuendo in his voice.

Yeah. Silly. What about them?

When they got to the hotel after what felt like an endless cab ride through the fog, Craig registered while she bought a magazine in a shop just off the foyer.

"We're in 410," he said, punching the elevator button.

They were both quiet during the ride up to the fourth floor. Temple was so aware of him standing next to her that she could hear him breathing. Never had she been so conscious of him. Her skin felt prickly. This was definitely not a brother-sister kind of feeling.

Craig unlocked the door of the room and flicked on the light. The room was plain but clean. Temple was relieved to see it had two beds.

"Double beds," Craig said, then began to empty his pockets. Change and keys rattled onto the nightstand.

Moving to the window, she pushed back the drapes and looked out. "I can hardly see the street now. It's like we're inside a ball of cotton."

"I think I'll call Neal."

"Who?"

"Neal. An old navy buddy who lives here. We get together at least once a month."

"If you're going to use the phone, I'm going to freshen up a little."

"Be my guest."

He reached for the phone as she closed the bathroom door.

When she emerged from the bathroom later, he was lying on the bed, sock-footed, watching "Another World."

"Soap operas?" she chided.

"Three channels, max. This isn't the Hilton."

Sitting down on her bed, Temple looked around the room. The Hilton it wasn't. Two double beds, a nightstand, a long vanity, TV and a straight-back chair.

"We've been invited to dinner."

She glanced up. "By whom?"

"Neal and his wife."

"Ummm." She leaned back against her pillow and closed her eyes. "You go. I'll be fine here."

"Three channels," he reminded. "It could be a long night."

She yawned. "What's on?"

Craig picked up the channel guide. "Let's see. A religious crusade, a telethon and...oh, this looks good. Reruns of the NBA playoffs—"

Rolling off the bed, Temple resignedly slipped her shoes back on.

"Don't look so glum," he said. "Neal's a great guy, and you'll like Maryann."

"Maryann?"

"Neal's Mrs. Right."

"I suppose they have one of those perfect marriages." That's all she needed. A night with a happily married couple in a cozy home to remind her of how good life could be with Mr. Right. The Mr. Right she couldn't seem to find.

"I suppose they do," Craig said absently, flipping through the three channels again.

What was it with men? she wondered. Did they think the programs were going to change just because they kept running through the channels?

NEAL WAS the same height as Craig, but blond to his dark hair, brown-eyed instead of blue-eyed. Maryann was a petite brunette who looked little more than sixteen years old, her age, she was quick to point out, when she'd met Neal.

The two men greeted each other heartily.

"Well, Flyboy, sorry about the fog, but it gave us a chance to get together. And who might this be?" he said, turning to Temple.

"Temple Burney." Craig made the introductions. "Neal and Maryann."

"I'm glad you could come," Maryann said, drawing Temple into the kitchen with her. "Now I'll have somebody to talk to while they swap war stories."

Temple liked Maryann immediately. It was impossible not to. Within five minutes, she was making a salad while Maryann fished steaks out of the marinade.

The kitchen was a charming country style, with gingham curtains at the window that overlooked a patio filled with flowering plants. Perfect house. Perfect couple.

This is what I'm searching for. Just have to find the right man and, this too, can be mine, Temple told herself.

"Neal, the grill's ready," Maryann sang out.

The two men passed through the kitchen, both talking at the same time.

"They're a pair." Maryann said fondly. "You'd think they were brothers. Neal, the grill is ready," she repeated sharply.

"I heard you, Maryann."

Temple glanced up at the censure in Neal's tone, but Maryann seemed unfazed.

"When those two were in the Persian Gulf, I don't know which I worried about more," Maryann said. "How long have you known Craig?"

"Since we were kids. We even went to summer camp together. We lost touch while he was in the service, but we both joined Sparrow Airlines five years ago and...the rest is history."

"He's never mentioned me or Neal?"

Temple thought about that a moment. "No." That seemed odd, too. Nancy was a closed subject, and now there was Neal and Maryann. It made her wonder what else Craig hadn't shared with her.

"Really? Neal, the grill is ready!" The veins in Maryann's neck stood out with the force of the reminder.

The door flew open, and Neal appeared. Shooting his wife an impatient glance, Neal snatched up the plate of steaks and left the room.

"Craig's talked about you," Maryann continued, seemingly oblivious to the tension in the air as Neal slammed out the back door.

Temple stopped washing carrots and looked out the window. Neal was putting the steaks on the grill while Craig bounced a basketball on the concrete patio.

"He has?"

"Uh-huh. He has dinner with us at least once a month. And we know about you two helping each other to find the perfect mate."

A cold knot of apprehension formed in Temple's stomach. "He told you about that?" What was the deal here?

"Uh-huh. He told us about Gabrielle and the cats episode." Suddenly, Maryann glanced up at her, desperation blazing in her eyes. "Don't do it."

"Pardon?"

Leaning closer, Maryann whispered quickly. "Take my advice and stay single. You've got it made and don't realize it."

Temple was confused. She'd only known Neal and
Maryann an hour but they seemed to have all the ingredi-
ents for a perfect marriage, certain tensions aside.

"But . . . you and Neal seem so perfect—"

"Looks are deceiving sometimes."

The back door opened and Neal stuck his head in.
"Where's the long fork?"

"Right here, darling." Maryann handed it to him with a
tense smile.

He slammed the door, making the curtain flop.

Maryann began chopping celery with wicked vigor. The
room was uncomfortably silent. Temple didn't know what
to say so she kept quiet until Neal's testy voice shattered the
silence.

"Steaks are ready!"

"If you like them still mooing," Maryann muttered.
"Turn mine over again," she shouted out the window.

Craig wandered in through the back door. Catching
Temple's puzzled look, he shrugged.

They sat down to eat ten minutes later.

"Dig in," Neal invited. "Steak sauce, Maryann."

"You're closer to the refrigerator, dear."

The couple's gaze locked in a tense duel.

"I'll get it," Temple offered.

"Sit down," Maryann ordered. "You're company."

Shoving back from the table, Maryann got the sauce out
of the fridge.

The meal got under way. The men conversed easily but
Maryann was silent, looking morosely at her plate. The
tension in the room was so thick Temple would have felt
more comfortable in a roomful of rattlesnakes.

Apparently, Neal and Maryann's marriage wasn't the icon
of bliss she'd thought. Her gaze met Craig's across the table, but he was either oblivious to the tension, or simply ignoring it.

"Monday went about the same," Craig was saying.
"Take off, climb through thirty thousand feet, lost cabin
control, head back. But this time, we picked up two me-

chanics who specialize in this cargo-door setup and spent a serious amount of time and fuel loitering around several states at FL310 trying to isolate this obvious loss of air from the cabin.

"You want thrills? Wait until you're at thirty-one thousand feet and some Marine mechanic starts pounding on your cargo door with a hammer and a block of wood."

Temple concentrated on her food as Craig and Neal continued with their war stories, listening to Craig's soft baritone that was so familiar. The idea that he kept things from her bothered Temple more than it should. Why hadn't he ever mentioned Neal and Maryann?

Neal reached for another roll. "I heard you got grounded the next week."

Craig laughed. "Well, that's the breaks. It seems that a captain had been trying to figure out what was wrong with this plane for a month and couldn't pinpoint it. When he found out what happened, he managed to get our orders changed and we were grounded for two weeks. The moral being, never show up your superior, even if you're right."

"Number-one rule." Neal chuckled.

Maryann stood up and abruptly began to clear the table, her lips compressed into a tight line. "Coffee?"

"Thank you," Temple accepted. "Can I help?"

"You better make it if you want to drink it," Neal said.

Maryann's eyes narrowed. "Is that a crack about my coffee?"

The couple's gaze locked again. The room pulsated with tension. Temple's gaze found Craig's. She could wring his neck for inviting her to witness this.

"No, it's a fact."

Temple cringed inwardly.

Maryann turned to Temple. "I'm very sorry, but I've suddenly developed a splitting headache. Will you excuse me?"

Craig stood up as she left the table.

Sitting back down, he glanced at Temple, who signaled him with her eyes it was time to leave.

A moment later, the water glasses on the table rattled as the bedroom door slammed shut.

Craig and Temple called a cab from the living room and waited on the front porch. When the cab deposited them back at the hotel, they stood watching the car's taillights disappear into the swirling fog, then looked at each other. Suddenly they both burst out laughing.

"That was interesting," Temple finally said when she could catch her breath.

"You think so?"

"Not really."

They stood in the square of light coming from the hotel doors, watching the fog eddy around them, reliving the uncomfortable episode.

"Steak sauce, Maryann!"

"You're closer, dear!"

Temple hooked her arm through Craig's as they finally went inside the hotel. After the fiasco they'd witnessed this evening, she had a new appreciation for his even temper. Never in her wildest imagination could she see him reacting as Neal had tonight, no matter how upset.

"Craig—"

"Hmm?"

"Why haven't you ever mentioned Maryann and Neal?"

"Just never thought about it," he said, pacing a step or two away in the lobby.

Temple digested that for a few moments.

"You knew they were having trouble, didn't you?"

"Would I subject you to an evening like this if I knew?"

She paused, studying him. "Yes, I think you would." It was suddenly clear what he'd done. "You were trying to make a point, weren't you?"

"The point being?"

Her gaze met his as she said, "That marriage is great if it's with the right person. Hell if it isn't."

Should I ask why it was important for him to make that point? Was he thinking about him and Nancy? Or me...and anybody I meet in haste?

"Well, it is a thought, don't you agree?"

As they waited for the elevator, Temple tried to sort out what he meant. Love wasn't something that could be rushed. As Grams said, it could happen at the most unexpected moment, and sometimes, with the most improbable candidate.

She was still thinking about that when the elevator arrived and they got in. This evening was an example of why Craig had broken his engagement to Nancy. He'd known it wasn't right. The problem was, Nancy didn't see it that way.

"You were right," she said at last. "I did like Maryann. She and Neal could have handled things a little better, though." She watched the numbers flash as the elevator moved upward. "Maybe we should ease up on finding Mr. or Ms. Right," she mused aloud. After tonight's debacle, single life looked pretty good to her.

Not saying a word, he drew her lightly into his arms. Taking advantage. She snuggled closer to his broad shoulder, feeling so content she suddenly laughed.

"What's so funny?"

"Me. Want to know what I thought when I met Neal and Maryann?"

"What?"

She buried her face in his shoulder, partly to smother another laugh, partly just because she wanted to. "Just think, Temple, you have only to find Mr. Right and this, too, could be yours.' "

9

A COLD RAIN had started falling, adding to the fog. It was so dreary outside that the dismal hotel room looked almost cheery.

"You think the fog will lift early?" she asked.

"It's hard to say."

Craig slipped the security lock on the hotel-room door and tossed the key onto the lamp table.

"Let's sleep in tomorrow morning," she suggested. Sleeping in was a luxury when they didn't have to be at the airport at five-thirty.

"I'll call the tower around five," he told her. "See how things stand." He shrugged out of his uniform jacket and hung it over the back of a chair. "I'm hungry."

"I think I have a granola bar in my purse."

"I'm not that hungry."

Stepping out of her pumps, Temple flexed her toes and sat down on the only chair in the room. "Maryann said that you'd mentioned me. How come?"

"Did I?"

"Maryann said you did."

"I might have mentioned you. Which bed do you want?"

"Right."

Stripping off his tie, he tossed it on the nightstand. He moved to the window and looked out, hands resting on his hips. The standard blue shirt stretched taut across his shoulders, tapering to his waist. He slowly started unbuttoning his shirt, and the room suddenly closed in on Temple.

Nancy, you're right. That is one gorgeous man.

The problem was, Nancy had never been able to forget Craig. Is that what would happen to her if she and Craig stopped being "best buddies"?

He was still framed by the window, his face all planes and angles in the dim light from outside. How was it that after a long day, and a frustrating evening, he still looked so damned attractive?

Temple tossed her shoes into the small closet. "I was thinking on the way home," she said. "I've known you for such a long time, and yet there are areas of your life that are a mystery."

He smiled and her heart double-timed. "What do you want to know?" he said. "The years I was in the navy? When I got out? What size shoe I wear? How I like my eggs?"

"Early to mid-eighties, called back up during the Gulf War, size eleven, scrambled," Temple said. "Why did you break up with Nancy?" The words were out before she realized it.

He looked up, his expression warning her he wasn't going to answer.

"I know it isn't any of my business, but she's never said— I just sort of wondered—" Was another woman involved? Another man?

"Do you two still have a close friendship?" he asked.

"We talk, occasionally."

He removed his shirt, walked to the closet and hung it on a hanger. "Nancy's one subject I don't want to discuss. The relationship is over, and we've both moved on."

He turned, his gaze holding hers momentarily.

"I have pajamas in my flight bag," he said in answer to the question she'd asked several hours earlier.

She wasn't sure whether she was disappointed or relieved that he'd changed the subject. Disappointed. She wanted to know. Relieved. She didn't want to know.

"Somehow, I can't picture you as the type to wear pajamas," she said suddenly, imagining him stretched out in the nude.

"I don't." The soft baritone of his voice reached deep inside her.

Temple tried not to read anything into the sexy innuendo.

"You take the top," he said. "I'll take the bottoms."

Not trusting her voice, she shrugged. He fished the pajamas out of his flight bag and tossed it to her. "I don't know about you, but I'm ready for bed."

If she hadn't known better, she would have sworn he'd smiled, but he turned away before she could be sure.

"I think I'll watch a little of the basketball playoffs," he told her a moment later.

Temple went into the bathroom and closed the door. Leaning against it, she closed her eyes and forced herself to breathe.

He sleeps in the buff. She knew what his well-toned body looked like. They'd swum together in enough hotel pools over the years. His daily workouts at the gym kept him in top condition and the trunks he wore left little to the imagination. She'd noticed the appreciative, lingering glances tossed his way from other women. But this was different. Very different.

Dear sweet heaven, help me make it through the night.

Shoving away from the door, she turned on the water and then studied her reflection in the mirror. Why was she suddenly dissecting Craig's every sentence, every look? Why was she imagining him in the nude? What had changed? Over the years, they'd shared many intimate details of their lives: attractions, relationships, broken hearts. She'd nursed him through the flu, and he'd babied her through the chicken pox two years ago. But she'd also been careful to keep a certain distance between them. It was her choice. Why then did it bother her so much that there were things he hadn't told her?

Because of Nancy? What else could it be?

Well, whether she liked it or not, something seemed to be changing in her. Suddenly, she wanted more than just friendship with Craig. But that scared her. What would happen if they were to take that next dangerous step, and things didn't work out? What would she do without him?

Hold on there, Burney. You're getting ahead of yourself. Be calm. Every time you react without thinking things through, you get in trouble. Just stop and think.

"Hey." Craig rapped on the bathroom door. "You going to stay in there all night?"

"Sorry. I'll hurry."

She took the pins out of her hair, then brushed it and pinned it up again. Stripping quickly, she slipped into the tub and sank into the steaming water until it reached her chin. After a moment, she sat up and creamed her face with lotion. Fortunately, the hotel had provided them with a small courtesy kit containing toothbrush, shaving cream and razor. Like all flight attendants, she carried her own personal essentials in a large purse for this sort of occasion. Drawing a deep breath, she sank deeper into the hot water.

"Craig?"

"Yeah?" His voice came from the other side of the door.

"Have you thought about getting married since? I mean . . . really."

"Yeah. I've thought about it."

"Well, why haven't you . . . done it."

For a moment, she knew he wasn't going to answer. She was pushing him on the subject, and you didn't push him. On anything.

"Right time, wrong woman. Right woman, wrong time."

The idea of Craig married, the father of two-point-two children was more than she cared to think about. And yet...

"Who was the right woman?"

He didn't respond right away and she wished she hadn't asked the question.

"Are you going to stay in there all night?"

Temple released a long breath of relief. She really didn't want to know who he might have loved enough to marry.

"Ten more minutes, max."

When she finally emerged, wearing Craig's pajama top, he was stretched out on the bed, fingers laced behind his head, watching TV. He looked comfortable, and very domesticated. Relaxed. It was obvious he wasn't disturbed about their spending the night together.

Craig glanced up as she came out. His gaze lightly traveled her shapely length. "Hello? Who is this goddess? Please introduce yourself."

"Ms. Burney, to you."

Keep it light, Temple. Light and friendly.

"You weren't kidding, were you?" she said.

"About what?"

"About not wearing pajamas. This top still had the price tag on it." She sat on the edge of the bed and began brushing her hair.

"I never kid. Your favorite movie is on."

"Which one?"

"The one with Doris Day and David Niven."

She frowned at the screen. "Which one?"

"The one where they have all these kids and he's a New York critic. They keep the youngest one in a cage with a lock on it—"

"*Please Don't Eat the Daisies.* And they don't keep the baby in a cage," she said. "Their family's expanded, and now the apartment is too small, so Doris Day keeps the child in a playpen, turned upside down."

He handed her the remote, and slid off the bed. "Tissues are over there for the sad parts. I'm taking a shower."

As the bathroom door closed, Temple curled up on the bed. Reaching for a pillow to cradle, she picked at the scratchy tag in the back of the pajama collar, but wasn't able to tear it loose. Finally giving up, she held the pillow close, immersing herself in the movie.

The sound of the running shower lulled her. In the background, she could hear David Niven talking to Doris Day. They were in a small, romantic Italian restaurant, hoping to recapture their flagging relationship. Why couldn't she find a guy with David Niven's sense of humor, his suave manner, his self-confidence. Someone like . . . Craig . . .

Her eyes drifted closed. Niven's voice became Craig's, Day's voice hers.

"Anyone ever tell you how sexy you look in pajama tops?" Gentle hands touched her hair and she stirred.

"Mmm, darling, give up the apartment and move to the country with me. The house is coming along beautifully—I have a part in the local play—we could use your guidance—I love you . . . our children need you—"

Lips gently brushed her forehead. "You're a squirrel. Go back to sleep."

"Mmm—you smell good enough to eat—"

Something warm touched her forehead, and she snuggled closer to the delicious scent. "You're welcome to be my guest anytime you like."

Footsteps moved away from the bed as a commercial came on. The volume immediately increased five decibels.

Startled, her eyes shot open and she blinked, momentarily disoriented.

"Did you say something?" Craig called from the bathroom.

She sat up, trying to sort reality from dream. Craig was standing in front of the bathroom mirror, drying his hair with a towel, his raised arms redefining his muscular chest. The pajama bottoms hung low on his hips. Her eyes focused on the thick mat of dark hair covering his chest. A confusion of emotions flooded her as pieces of her dream stubbornly clung to her consciousness. She had been dreaming, hadn't she?

Leaning around the corner, Craig asked, "Something wrong?"

"No. Well, uh, there's a tag on the collar of these pajamas—"

"Want me to get it out?"

"If you can. I can't reach it—"

As he approached, she caught the scent of soap and Old Spice.

"Nice legs, Burney."

Temple quickly drew the sheet up.

"Modest?" He grinned, a dimple appearing in his left cheek.

Craig Stevens was absolutely devastating. How could there ever be a wrong time or place—

"Turn around."

"Wh—what?"

"If you want me to get that tag out—"

"Oh."

Feeling like an idiot, she turned around, hoping her face wasn't as flushed as it felt.

His fingertips brushed her skin as he swept her hair aside then turned the collar to reach the tag. For a scant moment, her breathing grew shallow and she wished she hadn't asked him to help.

"Why are you so edgy tonight?"

"Just get the tag, Stevens."

His hands were warm against the nape of her neck and for one crazy moment she wished he would . . . Go away.

"There," he said. "A ragged job, but it's out." His fingertip sensuously smoothed her skin. "It's rubbed a raw spot."

His fingertips lingered longer than she thought healthy for her peace of mind, before he finally settled the collar back into place.

"Want me to put some cream on that?"

She made herself roll away from him.

"It'll be all right. Thanks." She shoved the covers back on her bed and settled deeper into the sheets. They were stiff and scratchy. The pillows were flat as pancakes, and the bed as cold as Siberia.

"Leave the light on in the bathroom, okay?" she said.

"Sure."

As he returned to the bathroom, Temple closed her eyes and covered her face with her hands.

You're a fool! It can't be anything more. Stop looking at him that way. He isn't blind. He can tell you're ogling him. It's embarrassing.

When Craig switched off the bedside lamp, she pretended to be asleep. The soft rustle of sheets when he got into bed grated on her raw nerves. After he'd finally settled himself, the quiet was so loud she could hear her own heartbeat.

"Penny for your thoughts."

His voice was disturbingly male in the darkness and her nerves tightened another notch. She pretended not to hear him. She wouldn't divulge her thoughts at this moment for a million dollars.

"Come on, you're not asleep. Remember? I know you never drop right off to sleep."

She resisted the desire to roll over. If she just ignored him . . .

He said nothing for a minute or two.

"Feels strange, doesn't it?"

"Yeah," she murmured, then realized he'd caught her.

They lay in the darkness, listening to the silence. She'd never felt quite so alone.

This, Grams, is what you keep telling me about. This kind of empty no-one-loves-me alone. No wonder you keep nagging at me to find someone.

"Ever thought about us?"

His question startled her. He was reading her mind! She nearly groaned aloud with embarrassment.

"You and me?" she asked as if she'd never given it a thought.

"You and me." His voice sounded deeply masculine . . . all sexy and alluring. "Ever wonder why we haven't—"

She waited for him to complete the sentence.

"Ever what?"

"Ever been like this before?"

She swallowed, wishing she could think of something clever or seductive to say. Doris Day always could. "Like what?"

"In a bedroom together."

Closing her eyes, she said softly, "We're just friends."

"You can't like a person and make love to them at the same time?"

Temple knew they were close to opening a Pandora's box that would set free all kinds of repercussions. Repercussions she wasn't sure she could handle without getting hurt, or hurting someone else.

"What we have in the... living room... is special."

"Yes, it is." He paused, then said softly, "But why wouldn't what we might have... in the bedroom... be as special?"

"Because 'that' could very well ruin 'this'."

"I disagree."

"I've seen it happen to other friends too many times."

"I have the feeling it could be very nice between us."

His voice was warm, husky, inviting. Nice? It could be heaven. She was as certain of that as her own name. But did they dare? Did *she* dare? Unable to lie still, she sat up and plunged her fingers into the tangle of her hair.

"Okay," he continued when she didn't say anything. "Think about this. Why can't two consenting adults enjoy each other's company?"

"Go to sleep," she said as she lay down again. She wanted more than superficial sex, especially with him.

The bed creaked when he turned over. He lay on his side in the near darkness and she could feel him looking at her.

Antsy, she turned over, then onto her back again.

"What's wrong?"

"I'm cold." Now that she wasn't having lustful thoughts about Craig, she'd noticed the temperature.

"Get another blanket."

"There isn't one. I looked."

Goose bumps dimpled her skin and she forced herself to breathe. Every ounce of her wanted him. Dammit!

His bare shoulders gleamed in the pale light and she could see the outline of his long body. She suddenly couldn't think of anything except how good it had felt when he'd drawn her against him in the elevator and how she had this insane urge to be held by him again. Hypocritical? You got it. Out of her mind? Clearly.

"Well, I guess that means you'll have to move over here so I can keep you warm."

The silence lengthened. The four feet between the beds seemed as wide as the Grand Canyon, and just as deep. She could hear the cold rain outside hitting the window and it made her even colder.

"Coming over?" he said. "I don't bite—unless I'm asked to." His voice and his words teased her.

"I hardly think so, not after what we've just been discussing."

A grin colored his voice. "Friends can't keep each other warm?"

Oh, he'd keep her warm all right. Red-hot. She wouldn't go over there if someone offered her the winning ticket in a lottery.

"You don't trust me?"

She couldn't trust herself. "I'll be fine in a few minutes."

"Suit yourself."

Time dragged on. Rain pelted the window. Twice she thought she heard sleet. Pulling the thin sheet and blanket closer around her, her teeth chattered.

A long time later, his voice came to her again in the darkness.

"I heard a story once about a man lost in a snowstorm. He shot a cow, gutted it and crawled inside the carcass to keep warm."

"Can't sleep, either?" she said.

"No, I'm cold, too."

"The cow story is interesting. Pointless, but interesting." She still wasn't moving to his bed.

Feet like ice cubes, she tried to force sleep. When sleet began pelting the window again, she surrendered.

Crawling out of bed, she dragged the blanket and sheet with her as she slid into bed with him.

"Scoot over," she whispered, nudging him. He scooted over without opening his eyes.

She stretched out carefully beside him, a full three inches between them, but his arms drifted around her and drew her close. Her back against his chest, his legs fitting against her, she pushed aside the idea that she was making a big mistake. Snuggling deeper against him, she savored his heavenly warmth. This was okay. Just for tonight it was okay.

"You certainly took long enough," he murmured, his breath warm against the side of her neck.

"It isn't capitulation," she mumbled back, "only an admission that I'm freezing and where the hell is a cow when you need one."

Holding each other close, they eventually dropped off to sleep.

Toward dawn, Craig opened his eyes, painfully aware of Temple's body cuddled next to his. She was snuggled against him, her hand resting on his chest, her knee lapped over his thigh. Her breath was soft and warm against his shoulder, like the touch of a feather. He breathed deeply, inhaling the scent of wildflowers. Suddenly, he had a sense of rightness. Temple lying next to him, warm and tantalizing.

Turning his head slightly, he let the sight of her silky auburn hair tangled across the pillow sink into him. He'd dreamed of this, fantasized about it. In his dream, however, there had been no pain shooting from wrist to shoulder. She was lying on his arm, cutting off circulation.

Easing up on the pillow, he carefully tried to free his arm. Sighing, she moved closer, her arm looping around his neck, her fingertips caressing him briefly. "Mmm," she murmured.

Oh, Lord.

"Sit up a little," he whispered, wincing as needles stung the inside of his arm.

"Mmm?" She shifted, following his warmth, turning half onto her back.

"Sit up..."

"Mmm..." She licked her lips, the tip of her tongue inviting.

They were within a breath of each other.

"Temple—"

Her soft breath feathered against his face.

It was too much.

Moving ever so slightly, he touched his lips to hers, lingering, tasting. With a soft sound, her mouth opened beneath his, kissing him back, soft, warm, clinging.

They'd never kissed before. Not like this. He'd never kissed anyone like this. Oh, he'd thought of it, but even in his dreams it hadn't been this sweet.

Easing her back against the pillow, he closed his eyes and coaxed her lips apart. Her mouth opened beneath his like an exotic flower. He took comfort that his circulation was working perfectly now. Working very well, in fact. The ache in his groin was a living, growing entity.

She moved against him and a flash of heat rushed through him. The kiss deepened, her hand resting on the nape of his neck, and the heat became a searing ache. Her purr of pleasure fueled his passion. This... this was what had kept him awake all night. Thinking of this, wondering if reality could possibly live up to the dream. It did.

Pressing her into the pillow, his fingers struggled with the buttons of the pajama top, but the tangle of sheets and blanket impeded his progress.

Impatient, he ripped aside the blankets, his mouth devouring hers now. She clung to him, her hands moving over him, molding his shoulders, sliding over his chest. His pulse pounded in his veins when her nails lightly scored his skin.

But suddenly, as quickly as she had come to him, she retreated.

Sighing softly, she rolled over and snuggled more deeply into the bed. Stunned, his breath caught in his throat, his nerves screaming, she settled into the even breathing of deep sleep.

Rolling onto his back, he jammed his fingers through his hair and clasped his hands to his head as he stared at the ceiling. His nerves were screaming, his need insistent. Damn, but he wanted her.

What now?

He studied her sleeping face, cataloging every shadow, every angle. Would she ever realize . . .

Lately, he'd begun to hope she'd noticed things changing between them, but if she had, she'd hidden it well. Until tonight. She'd been as on edge as he, and he knew why. The problem was, what to do about it.

Temple turned over again. The too-large pajama top gaped open, exposing the first curve of a luscious breast. He couldn't resist the temptation to let his fingertips drift across that curve. Her lips parted invitingly. It was too much.

Easing onto his side, he pulled her beneath him. His arms resting on either side of her tousled head, his mouth brushed across hers, again lingering, tasting. When she responded, moving beneath him, reaching for him, he knew she might still be half-asleep, but she knew exactly what she was doing.

She responded wickedly, whispering his name, "Craig . . . Craig," as her fingers released the snap on his pajamas. The groan her touch evoked was smothered by more lingering kisses.

She had to be awake.

Pajamas tops and bottom hit the floor, caught in a tangle of blankets and sheets in a flurry of need. Impatient murmurs punctuated low assent as hands and mouths searched bare skin. Everything he'd been denying for months flooded through him. She fit against his body perfectly. She responded to him like half of himself, anticipating, initiating. Driving him crazy. It was too late to think. Far too late to turn back.

Tomorrow he'd worry about friendship.

Passion seized him, and all rational thought fled.

10

IT WAS PAST FIVE when Craig stirred. Sitting up, he squinted at the illuminated dial on the clock. When he saw the time, he reached for the phone. The tower advised him the fog wouldn't be lifting until late morning.

Rolling over, he drew Temple to him before falling back to sleep. This was good. Very good.

It was late when they woke again.

"What time is it?"

"Um, nine," he said.

She stretched lazily, feeling warm and good. "Let's not get up yet."

"Roger."

They lay there together, half-asleep, talking softly. It felt right, comfortable.

Craig liked having her beside him in bed. She looked like a little girl in the morning—eyes drowsy, hair tousled, lips pink and inviting. Too damn inviting.

Temple gave no indication that she remembered last night. Though he wanted to share with her how good it had felt to hold her, to make love with her, it seemed she wasn't ready to do that. It had to be the pilot thing. She'd always been so adamant about not having romantic relationships with pilots.

Well, he'd let her think about how last night changed things and see what developed. If their relationship changed from friendship to something more, it was up to her—at least for now. But he'd only wait so long.

Around ten, they went downstairs to the hotel restaurant for breakfast. Over pancakes and sausages, the conversation was so normal Craig began to wonder if he had dreamed the encounter, but each time their gazes met and hers skipped away, the tightening in his groin told him he hadn't imagined anything. Take it easy, he reminded himself. Go slow and see what happens.

"So, what's on your docket when we get back?" he said lightly as he finished his pancakes and speared his last sausage.

"I'm off for a few days. I think I'll go visit Grams."

"When will you be back?"

"Maybe never." She sighed. "But most likely Friday." She ate the last of her pancakes, grinning. "I know. You'll miss me unbearably, and live for the moment I return. You're envious of Neal and Maryann and you want a marriage just like theirs."

Not one word about the night before. Nothing.

He lifted his coffee cup in a mock salute, careful not to let his frustration show. "Hurry back."

EARLY THE NEXT MORNING, Temple made the three-hour drive to Summersville, arriving late in the afternoon. It was Wednesday and, knowing Grams would be at the church, she decided to go there first.

The choir was practicing as Temple slipped into a back pew. The stained glass lining the windows filled her with a sense of peace, though she felt anything but peaceful.

The twelve choir members were intent on their music, their voices following the rise and fall of Eleanor Liddy's hands. Elevated on a small platform, Grams sang along with the choir, her strong alto blending harmoniously with the others.

As the organ music faded, Eleanor turned and spotted her granddaughter. Her face lit up. "Tootie!"

Hands extended, Grams made her way down the aisle, a radiant smile creasing her weathered face. "What a wonderful surprise."

"Hello, Grams." Tears of love stung Temple's eyes as she hugged her grandmother.

"Alta, Bertha, Virginia, come meet my granddaughter," Eleanor called to her friends in the choir loft.

The small group disbanded and three elderly ladies about Grams's age, each with the same shade of gray-purple hair, made their way out toward her.

"We've heard so much about you, dear," one greeted.

"My, yes. Eleanor says you lead such an exciting life!" the other chirped. "You're a flight attendant?"

"I am." Temple smiled warmly, grasping frail, blue-veined hands in both of hers.

"Oh, my, how exciting," they said enthusiastically. "Handsome, exciting men all around you!'

"Oh, my, yes!" Temple exclaimed, then thought, *if you only knew.*

On the drive to Grams's cottage, Temple reacquainted herself with the sights. Summersville, with its two-story homes with large wraparound porches and blooming flower boxes reminded Temple of Mayberry, USA. What had to be the last dime store in the nation, Fenney's Five-and-Dime, was still open for business on the corner of the square. A bird-covered statue of some forgotten general stood in the center of town. Sixty-year-old elms and maples lined narrow streets that had once carried Model T cars—some roads still had cobbled surfaces. Nine churches, three city parks with pavilions where the city celebrated a variety of July the Fourth celebrations. Middle America. The heartbeat of a nation. Her own heartbeat.

Each time she came home, it felt good. Peaceful. Or was it simply that Grams living here made it feel that way? The big, two-story house where Temple had been raised had been torn down and a public parking lot erected. Several years earlier, Grams had decided the house was too big for one person, so she'd sold it and bought a small, ivy-covered cottage closer to church.

Temple sat at the familiar round claw-footed table in her grandmother's kitchen and ate chocolate chip cookies—the same recipe Temple had been making for Craig for ten years.

Craig.

Suddenly losing her appetite, she laid the cookie aside, and reached for the glass of milk Grams had set in front of her.

"Now then," Grams said as she settled herself. "Want to tell me what's bothering you?"

"Nothing's bothering me. I just wanted to see you."

"I'm always delighted to see you," the older woman said. "It's always much too long between visits. Now, stop stalling and tell me what brings you all the way down here without the excuse of a holiday?"

Grams had always been able to see right through her.

Sighing, Temple broke off a piece of cookie. "You know me too well."

"I love you." She patted Temple's hand. "You always find peace here, don't you, Tootie?"

"Sometimes I wish things were like they were fifty years ago. Plain. Fundamental," Temple said.

Grams laughed. "Life wasn't easier when I was young, just different. The judge and I had our problems. Men, women, sex. When to do it, when not to do it. The proper time, the right man. No less weightier issues now than they were then."

"I—" Temple didn't know what to say.

"Tootie, darling, your grandfather was my first love, my only love. But it didn't mean we had no problems," Grams said gently. "Your parents had their own set of troubles— your mother especially, after your father... didn't come back. Women have had problems with relationships with men from the beginning of time. And I'd say, by that worried look in your eyes, you're knee-deep in man trouble. Now, tell me what's brought you all the way to Summersville in the middle of the week."

"Oh, Grams, I think I made a big mistake," Temple said sadly.

"Well, mistakes can be corrected."

"I don't know if this one can be."

"Well, tell me about this mistake you made, and we'll see how monumental it is."

"A man, a pilot—we've been friends for years—"

"Craig Stevens."

"How did you know?"

"You talk about him in every letter. Go on for several pages at a time, if I recall." Leaning back, Eleanor smiled. "I haven't seen him in years, but as I recall, he was a knockout, even in his youth."

"Grams!"

"What? I may be old, but I can still dream, can't I?"

"Craig and I are the best of friends. He's like...part of me." It was difficult to admit, but it was true. "Our best times are when we're together. We always have something to talk about. We share the same interests. It's just...a very comfortable friendship."

"Doesn't sound like the worst thing that could happen to a woman."

Temple toyed with her glass, trying to form the proper words. After a few moments, she said, "A couple of nights ago, we got fogged in during one of our flights."

Grams nodded, her eyes bright with comprehension.

Recognizing her assumption, Temple groaned. "I haven't finished."

"You don't need to."

"I'm in love with him, Grams," she admitted miserably. Saying it aloud let the words sink into her heart, a place she'd carefully protected—until two nights ago.

"Oh," Grams reached for another cookie. "And this is the monumental problem?"

Temple buried her fingers in her hair, massaging her temples with the heels of her hands. "I don't want to be in love with him. I want things to stay the way they are—were," she amended.

Grams's eyes softened with understanding. "Why, Tootie, when you love him?"

"I don't want to risk our friendship by muddying the waters with...other things." Sex, she might have said but didn't. Wonderful, glorious, uninhibited, hot sex. "He's too important to me."

"How does Craig feel about the matter?"

"I don't know. We haven't discussed it."

Grams lowered her cup. "You haven't discussed it?"

"It just happened, Grams...and I was a coward. The next morning, I avoided the subject. Pretended I didn't... remember."

Grams's eyebrows arched. "Did wonders for his ego, I'm sure." She smiled reassuringly. "It does appear you have a dilemma."

Temple sighed. "What am I going to do? Craig's not only my best friend, he was once engaged to one of my closest friends. The relationship didn't work, but Nancy's still carrying a torch for him."

"If Craig's relationship with Nancy didn't work out, why should Nancy's feelings be of immediate concern to you?"

"You know me, Grams," Temple said. "I feel guilty petting somebody else's dog. How can I face Nancy knowing that I'm in love with Craig and she is too."

"My," Grams said. "The plot thickens."

"Does it ever. Like glue."

They talked straight through dinner, and then long into the evening. It wasn't that Temple had so much to say but that suddenly she had so much to learn from her grandmother. She'd always thought of Grams and cookies and hot tea. Now, all of a sudden, she discovered that Eleanor had a wealth of insights about relationships.

Later that evening, Temple lay in bed in her old room under the eaves, but she didn't sleep well that night. Nor the next. Dreams laced with erotic memories of Craig kept her awake. Friday morning found her hollow-headed and fuzzy.

"Didn't sleep well again?"

Grams, dressed in her nubby robe, her hair in curlers, bustled around the kitchen making French toast.

"Not really—Grams, it's so early. You didn't have to get up and see me off." It wasn't yet 4:00 a.m.

"Nonsense. I wanted to. Feeling better about Craig?"

"Worse," Temple admitted. He was right. Sometimes things didn't fit—right man, wrong time.

"Well, at least you're starting to be honest with yourself," Grams said as she turned the bacon. "In the Dark Ages, when I was a young woman trying to decide what I wanted from life, I made a few mistakes. Nothing very life-changing, but nevertheless things that made me stop and think. Maybe that's why you were fogged in with Craig the other night—to make you both think." She glanced up, smiling. "Two or three pieces of bacon, dear?"

After breakfast, Temple started back to Dallas for her eight o'clock flight. Nothing had been resolved, but she felt a little better. And she felt closer to Grams than ever before.

Arriving at the terminal a few minutes early, Temple parked the truck in her best lane-shark manner. Craig was nowhere in sight this morning.

Good. One less problem to start the day off.

Entering the building, she headed straight for the lunch counter, where Flo was just getting ready to sit down.

"Wow." Flo looked her over with a knowing eye. "Bad week?"

"Bad life. Slept badly. Headache," she lied, sliding onto a stool at the counter. "Coffee emergency."

Ginny poured two cups as Flo sat down, lighting a cigarette. "Heard you were fogged in with Stevens the other night. Anything interesting happen?"

Temple eyed Flo over the rim of her mug. "What makes you think there would be?"

"Oh, I don't know. Maybe the fact that he doesn't look any better than you?"

Temple froze, realizing Flo was looking into the mirror hanging behind the lunch counter.

Half turning, Temple caught sight of Craig from the corner of her eye. "He's wearing sunglasses. How can you tell what he looks like?"

"He's been moping around like a neutered cat all week," Flo said. "What happened between you two the other night?"

"Nothing. We had dinner with friends."

"Yeah. And?"

Ginny leaned across the counter. "Come on, spill your guts."

Temple concentrated on her coffee cup. "There's nothing to spill. We had dinner with some friends of his, went back to the hotel and went to bed."

"Yessss!" Flo crowed, her fist punching the air.

"And went to sleep. Nothing happened. Satisfied?"

"If you were."

Temple didn't like the direction this conversation was taking, but she couldn't think of a way to divert it without drawing more attention to the subject. And that was the last thing she needed, more questions.

"Craig isn't interested in me—he—he—" she said the first thing that popped into her mind "—likes my cookies."

Flo grinned. "Does he ever."

"Cookies, my foot," Ginny said. "I've seen the way he looks at you and cookies are the last thing on that man's mind."

"You ought to get this 'friend' thing out of your head," Flo added. "What's wrong with being lovers?"

"Excuse me," Temple said suddenly. "I have to run. I'm late for my flight." Sliding off the stool, Temple reached for her flight bag.

"Coward," Ginny accused.

"Cookies," Flo scoffed. "I'll bet."

Once Temple was on board, she checked the galley, started coffee, then walked through the cabin. Craig and Bruce Dumont were in the cockpit finishing the preflight checks when she stepped inside. "Coffee?"

"You're a lifesaver," Bruce said, taking a cup while keeping his attention on his clipboard and gauges.

"Brakes."

"Applied and set," Craig said, also taking a cup.

"Mixture."

"Full rich."

Craig sipped his coffee. "Have a good time at Grams's?"

"Wonderful, thank you. I know I've gained ten pounds on all the French toast, mashed potatoes, pot roast and gravy I ate."

Craig's eyes skimmed her trim figure. "I don't think so."

"Flaps."

"Check."

There wasn't the usual banter this morning, but Temple told herself it was because they were running behind schedule. Taking her cue, she exited the cockpit and returned to the galley.

The day went without incident, and they landed back in Dallas around six-thirty.

She wasn't hiding from Craig. Why should she? Nevertheless, she went straight home from work.

Thumbing through her mail as she rode the elevator to her apartment, Temple stopped when she saw the familiar scrawl on a yellow envelope.

"Nancy," she told the empty car.

Thumbing open the envelope, she scanned the short letter.

"Oh, brother," she breathed.

Talk about bad timing. Nancy was coming to Dallas for a couple of days to see friends and wanted to have dinner with her one evening. Nancy would have a million questions about Craig—who he was seeing being the principal one.

She wished... What did she wish? That Craig wasn't a pilot? That Nancy wasn't a friend? That she felt more secure about pilots? That she wished Nancy would forget about Craig? Fat chance. That she could forget she and Craig had made love and it had been nothing short of fantastic? Impossible.

She entered her apartment and threw Nancy's letter onto the desk, unwilling to deal with the visit and the questions tonight. Tonight she'd think about something, anything but Craig Stevens.

When the evening dragged on, she decided to do laundry. She'd finished two loads and had the first in a dryer, when a male tenant shouldered his way into the laundry room.

"Hi," he said, setting his clothes basket on a washer.

"Hi," she returned idly, thumbing through the latest issue of *People*.

From the corner of her eye, she watched him stuff clothes into the washer and wondered why it was that the mechanics of doing laundry escaped most men. They could tell you how an engine ran, or build jet planes, but sorting whites from coloreds? They went into a mental blackout.

Her dryer buzzed and she tossed the magazine back onto the cluttered wire table in the corner.

"I've never been able to get my clothes dry in less than three tries," he said.

She glanced over her shoulder. The man was stuffing jeans and whites into a second washer.

"I've tried them all," he said. "They have them set on low to prevent dummies like me from melting the elastic in their shorts."

Temple had to smile. He did have a certain charm, and was rather nice-looking.

He held out his hand. "Brian Baker. 4-D."

"I've seen you in the lobby," she said, returning his handshake. "Temple Burney. 3-A."

"You're the stewardess?"

"We're called hosts and hostesses now."

"Sorry."

"It's okay. The men resent the 'stewardess' tag."

He had the grace to laugh and she liked the sound of it. By the time they'd both finished their laundry, he'd asked for her phone number. She'd given it to him and they'd made a date for drinks the next night. Why not? Anything to keep her from thinking of Craig. And maybe she and Brian would hit it off.

Temple suggested they meet at a popular watering hole.

The best way to get one man off my mind is to see another one, she decided. And she wanted Craig off her mind.

ARRIVING A FEW MINUTES early the following evening, Temple took a seat at the bar. Brian arrived right on time and she waved to get his attention.

Two marks for him. He hadn't made her wait, and he was dressed neatly in charcoal slacks, a casual jacket, shirt open at the neck. No gold chains or bracelets. Nice.

Fresh start, Temple. This one has promise.

"I'm not late, am I?"

"Not at all." She caught a whiff of his cologne. An expensive, woodsy blend that was distinctive but not overpowering.

He ordered a drink. "This is nice."

"It is," Temple said. Her decision was on target. Remain friends with Craig, look for Mr. Right elsewhere. Might his name be Brian?

The bartender brought Brian's drink, he sipped it and settled himself more comfortably on a bar stool, his knees bumping hers. She felt nothing other than the bump, but it was too early. Lust took time.

They chatted for a while, making small talk. He seemed intelligent and well versed in current affairs. They ordered another round of drinks.

Getting more comfortable, he smiled at her over his glass. "This is going well. So maybe we should get a few things out of the way."

She studied his intense face. "Pardon?"

"Let's lay some ground rules."

She sipped her drink, hope starting to recede. But maybe not. "Okay."

"Well, for starters, what are your religious preferences?"

"Pardon?" She smiled. "I thought that was a subject to be avoided, especially on first dates."

"I'm different. What're your religious convictions?"

"Well, I was raised Catholic—"

His glass smacked smartly against the bar and she flinched.

"Catholic?" he roared. He leaned close. "And I suppose you're a Republican to boot." A vein bulged in his neck. "Are you willing to let those hard-nosed conservatives suck you dry?" He downed his drink in one swallow. "Hell, I can see this is hopeless."

I'm not even willing to have this conversation, Temple thought. Drink halfway to her mouth, she watched Brian storm out of the bar. Thumbing her nose at his retreating back, she took a sip of her drink.

"Jerk," she murmured.

She turned and found the bartender watching her. She shrugged and he grinned.

"Well," she said, reaching for her purse, "I'm glad we didn't get around to money."

The bartender chuckled.

"I thought I'd have to hand you a bar towel and call a cab."

"Me? Cry over a blind date?" She tossed a ten on the bar. "I'm a veteran of hellish dates."

11

"BECKY, I've had it. I've sworn off blind dates," Temple said. She balanced the phone between her chin and shoulder as she pulled a sheet of cookies out of the oven and kneed the door shut.

"No.

"No!

"Your cousin?"

She slid the cookies onto a cooking rack.

"How long will he be in town?"

She didn't want to go out with anybody's cousin visiting from Philadelphia, but how could she say no? Becky was a good friend. She'd filled in for her when she was out with the flu last year.

"Okay." She sighed. "As long as we double."

They made arrangements for Becky and Bob, along with Becky's cousin, Ricky, to pick Temple up at seven-thirty that evening.

"You look smashing!" Becky exclaimed when Temple opened the door.

The rust-colored heavy silk pants suit—straight-legged trousers and long shirt—wasn't new. She wasn't about to waste good money on a new outfit in the vain hope of snagging Becky's cousin. She'd pulled her hair on top of her head in loose curls and wore gold hoops in her ears, but that was the only concession she'd made to glamour.

"The guys are waiting downstairs."

"Okay, tell me what I need to know about this cousin of yours."

"Well, we only see him at family reunions—"

Temple stopped, one shoe on and one shoe off. "You only see him every five years?"

"Every two," Becky corrected. "My side of the family goes to Philadelphia every other year."

"Becky—"

"Oh, it's okay," she assured Temple. "He's just like my uncle Randall. A real hoot. Has a good time wherever he is." She laughed at Temple's anxious look. "Oh, come on, silly. It'll be a fun evening. Come on, the men are waiting."

Feeling she should have stuck to her vow, Temple shoved her driver's license, some change and a small makeup bag into a minuscule purse that matched her suit, and followed Becky downstairs.

Ricky Lawrence was six to eight inches taller than Temple, and beefy like the ex-football player he was. Square face, brown eyes, thinning light brown hair and a crooked grin.

"Well, Temple girl, I'm happy to meet you!" he said, pumping her hand. "Becky said you were gorgeous." Her hand was lost in his enthusiastic grip.

"Hi, Temple," Bob called from the front seat of the car. "We've got reservations at Antonio's in twenty minutes."

Antonio's? Remembering her last experience there, she mentally groaned. She was eating spaghetti no matter what.

On a Friday night, Antonio's was always crowded, so they went into the bar to wait for their table. Temple prayed no one recognized her from the last visit.

Ricky ordered a Scotch and Bob a beer. Becky and Temple ordered white wine.

"Look at that!" Ricky bopped Temple's arm good-naturedly. "Football highlights!"

"Yeah...how about that." Temple reached for her wineglass.

The TV above the bar was showing bloopers, the missed touchdowns, the mistakes that made the game tolerable for Temple. "Becky tell you I played for Detroit?" Ricky said, his gaze pinned to the TV. "Running back."

"Oh? What do you do now?"

"Insurance. Look at that! Flipped that quarterback right on his butt." He punched her on the forearm again.

Two men at the bar turned, recognizing Ricky.

"Hey," one said, coming over, "aren't you—"

"Ricky Lawrence." Ricky stuck out his hand.

"Yeah! I thought so. Never understood why the Lions cut you. Man, you were a runnin' machine!"

A second man joined them and in a few minutes the four men were deep into football conversation.

Becky shrugged apologetically. "This is the way it always is," she said. "Somebody recognizes him and everything else is forgotten. That's why I wanted you to come along. At least I've got somebody to talk to."

Temple caught snatches of the men's conversation while she and Becky chatted. Rebecca Winter had been a flight attendant until little Cindy was born eight months earlier. Temple had hosted her baby shower. Though Becky had resigned, they still saw each another frequently.

"She's just a delight," Becky was saying. "I never knew how much a baby would change our lives. We thoroughly enjoy her." Becky sipped her wine. "Are you ever going to get married, Temple?"

Temple managed a laugh. "First I have to find the right man."

"Are you looking?"

"Yes, Becks, I'm looking."

"Ricky's a good catch," Becky said candidly.

"I don't know anything about football," Temple said, "and Philadelphia is too cold in the winter."

"He doesn't play football anymore."

A burst of laughter erupted as someone delivered a punch line. Turning around, Ricky hit Temple on the shoulder jovially and ordered another Scotch.

"Johnson, party of four. Johnson party of four."

"Bob." Becky grabbed her husband's arm, trying to get his attention. "Our table's ready."

"Hey, man," one of the fans shouted to Ricky, "it was good to talk to you!"

"Later, dude!" Ricky called back. "I don't run into many who saw that last game."

"It's too bad about the knee—" The besotted fan was reluctant to let him go.

Becky leaned closer to Temple once they were seated at their table. "Ricky injured a knee the last game he played. It didn't heal well and the Lions cut him the next season. It about killed him. Football's been his life, ever since he started with Mighty Mites in second grade." Her teeth worried her lower lip. "I hope those men didn't stir up painful memories. Ricky's rather sensitive about the subject...."

Oh, great. Ricky's "sensitive."

"When did he hurt his leg?" Temple asked.

"Two years ago, maybe three."

"That's too bad."

Becky eyed the hangers-on resentfully. "I hope these guys take the hint and go back to the bar."

Eventually they did, and the two couples turned to the menu.

The waiter approached. "May I get you something from the bar?"

"Nothing for me," Temple said, scanning the menu.

"Double Scotch," Ricky ordered, shoving his empty glass toward the waiter.

Bob and Ricky continued the conversation that had started in the bar. Words like *slot back* were mentioned and Becky rolled her eyes in exasperation.

"Whenever these two get together, all they talk about is football. Tell me why you've suddenly sworn off the dating circuit."

"I'm not off it, exactly," Temple told her friend. "But no more blind dates."

"Yeah, they can be beasts."

"I think I'm cursed. Perfectly normal men turn into weirdos when they're out with me."

Becky's eyes widened. "Seriously?"

"Seriously. An accountant figured our bill on a napkin—four times. Then there was the health nut—into garlic, thought it cured everything." Temple shuddered, recalling that night. "He 'healed' a whole theater the night we went out.

"I've paid for dinner so many times I'm about over my credit card limit. Actually, I can't afford to look for Mr. Right."

Ricky, suddenly recalling she was there, turned from his conversation with Bob to punch her on the forearm again. By now it was getting blue from the good-natured shots. "Doin' okay, Cupcake?"

"Fine, thank you. And my name is Temple."

Becky laughed as Ricky turned back to Bob. "Don't mind him. He gets a little distracted when he talks football."

Football reigned the conversation until dessert when Bob and Becky began discussing renovations on their old house.

Ricky ordered another drink.

Ten o'clock rolled around. Temple was looking at her watch. The subject was back to football. She was ready to go home.

"Another wine, Cupcake?" Temple dodged as Ricky aimed a fist at her shoulder and missed.

"Ricky, I think Temple wants to go home," Becky admonished.

"Home!" He peered closely at his watch. "It's only...ten o'clock."

"That late?" Temple quipped, aware Ricky'd been so busy drowning his "sensitivity," he'd lost track of time. "I really should be going."

"Sure thing. Waiter! Another Scotch, please!"

Ten dragged into eleven, eleven into twelve. The group moved to the adjoining bar. Temple and Becky sat on high-back stools with their hands under their chins, listening to football stories. The cleaning crew worked around them.

Deep into a story, Ricky stood up, reached for the first thing that resembled a football to make his point and threw it to the loyal fans who still lingered at the bar. The "football" was Temple's purse.

The small bag sailed across the bar and landed in a bucket of dirty mop water.

The men at the bar burst out laughing. "Missed the pass! Sorry!"

Laughing, Ricky started to sit back down when he lost his balance and fell against a waitress carrying a tray of empty pitchers and glasses.

Temple sprang out of her seat as the tray came crashing down, flinging half-empty glasses of beer, pieces of limes and decorative drink umbrellas at her.

Grabbing a napkin, she tried to sop up the sticky garbage from the front of her silk blouse.

"You need a little fancier footwork, Cupcake!" Ricky laughed, and the men at the bar roared.

"Bob, we have to go. The baby-sitter will think we left town," Becky complained when the ruckus got louder. The waiter returned to hand Temple her purse, which was soaking wet.

"Okay, sweetheart." Bob winked at Ricky. "Gotta run. The ole ball and chain has spoken."

Ricky glanced over at Temple, trying to focus. "Should have a woman like...like...Cupcake here. She's a real sport!"

Wincing, Temple took the forthcoming shot to the forearm in stride.

The men finally paid the bill, and they left the restaurant.

Hooking his arm around Temple's neck, Ricky walked her to the car.

"Hey, you and I have barely had time to talk," he said. "Go for a nightcap with me."

"Sorry, I have an early flight in the morning."

"Good idea, Ricky," Becky seconded amid Temple's spirited protests. "You two haven't had a chance to get to know each other."

Temple shot her an impatient look. Before she could stop him, Ricky hailed a cab.

He squeezed the back of her neck. "We'll just stop off for a little nightcap, then I'll see you home."

She sent Becky a desperate look, but Becky was already in the car. Waving goodbye, she and Bob drove off.

"Would you mind dropping me by my apartment," Temple said as he opened the door of the cab for her.

"Sure thing. After our nightcap. One drink, and you're on your way."

Aware of the condition of her stained clothing, she tried again. "Ricky, I'd rather not be seen in this condition."

"What condition? You look great! Besides, the place we're going is practically empty at this hour." He got in, gave the driver an address, then sat back, stretching his arm over the back of her seat.

"This is fun, huh?" he said expansively.

"Wonderful," she said lamely.

The cab pulled up in front of a small cocktail bar in a part of town Temple wasn't familiar with.

"They know me here," Ricky reassured her as they got out. "Friends of mine own the place. Used to play against 'em."

Personally autographed pictures of football players covered half of one wall. Ricky waved to the bartender as he directed Temple to a back table against the "glory wall." It was nearing 1:00 a.m., but the bar was crowded with ex-football players and their wives or girlfriends.

"What do you want?" Ricky asked, his gaze skimming over the crowd.

To disappear, Temple thought.

"Nothing, thanks."

"One Scotch," he ordered when a little blonde in three-inch heels and wearing minuscule shorts and crop top made her way to the table.

"Sure thing, hon," the waitress said and minced off.

"Ricky!" a solid wall of muscle called out, making his way to their table.

Ricky jumped up. "Buck-o!" The two pounded backs in greeting, nearly toppling the small table.

Steadying the table, Temple gritted her teeth.

"What are you doin' in town?" the wall of muscle asked.

"Got a cousin who lives here!" Ricky said. "Just down for a couple of days, checkin' out a few things."

"God, it's great to see you. You still in Philly?"

"Yeah, thought you were going to come see me!" The men pounded each other on the back again.

The waitress brought their drinks. Ricky quickly downed his and ordered another one. "Hey! There's Demon! What's he doin' down here! Hey, Demon!"

He got up, stumbling over the table in his haste to cross the room.

Another round of back-thumping followed and now three hulking men sat knee-to-knee at the tiny table.

"Men, this is . . . Cupcake. She's a stewardess for some bird airline."

"Hi, Cupcake," the two former football players echoed in unison.

A while later, Temple glanced at her watch. Ricky had spent the last twenty minutes reminiscing with old friends who dropped by the table. So much for small talk on their part.

"Ricky," she shouted to get his attention.

He turned, looking over his shoulder. "What?"

"It's late. I've got a flight in the morning—"

"Yeah, hold on."

She waited another ten minutes, then got his attention again.

"I've got to go—"

"Hey, I'm with my friends here—"

He'd had too much to drink and his tone was surly now. Clearly, he thought she was interfering with a good time.

"Fine. I'll call a cab—"

The conversation around the table stilled.

"One more drink," he said, his eyes trying to focus. The jukebox was so loud they had to shout to be heard.

"I want to go home now."

"Hold your britches, Cupcake. Barkeep, one for the road!"

Knowing that arguing with him would only create a bigger scene, Temple got up and edged her way from behind the table as the jukebox struck up "Kung Fu Fighting." The men were so deep into their drinks they never saw her leave.

As she exited the bar, Ricky had climbed up to the middle of the table, had stripped his shirt off and was pumping iron to the beat of the music. *It's your own fault, Cupcake. Once again you should have listened to your intuition,* Temple reminded herself as she trudged to a nearby all-night convenience store.

"Where's the phone?" she asked the clerk.

Eyeing her stained blouse, he pointed to the corner.

She'd call a cab, go home and forget this ever happened, she decided. But when she opened her purse, her spirits sank. She'd left her money at home. All she had was some wet change—mad money, Grams called it. A couple of quarters for a pay phone in case she got in trouble.

With grim resignation, she pushed one of the quarters into the pay phone and dialed . . .

A sleepy voice answered on the third ring.

"Stevens."

"Craig, it's Temple."

"Temple?" Craig's tone changed. "What's the matter."

She closed her eyes against tears. "I need you to come get me."

Wide-awake now, he sat up in bed, frowning at the clock. It was 2:00 a.m.

"Where are you?"

"I—I don't know where I am. Just a minute."

He could hear her talking to someone in a muffled tone.

"I'm at a convenience store at Third and Elm."

His mind worked quickly. Third and Elm. "What in the hell are you doing out there at a convenience store at this hour of the night?"

"Do you honesty need to ask?"

"Are you okay?"

"Fine. Just come and get me."

"I'm on my way."

Craig jerked on his jeans and jammed his feet into tennis shoes at the same time. He grabbed a shirt and pulled it on over his head with one hand while jamming keys and change into his pockets with the other.

The drive should have taken thirty minutes but he made it in eighteen. The Lincoln skidded to a stop at the curb and he jumped out before it stopped rocking.

Temple stood just inside the door of the store, her face white and anxious. She stepped outside when she saw him. Their eyes met, and she shrugged.

"What's going on?"

Brushing past him, she got into the front seat of the Lincoln and slammed the door.

Craig got in the driver's side and looked over at her worriedly.

"I'm...okay," she said. "Please, just take me home and don't ask questions."

He pulled way from the curb and drove down the street. The blue and red lights of police cars flashed brightly as he passed Spanky's Bar. She sank lower in the seat as a primal voice shouted, "CUPCAKE! WHERE ARE YOU?"

Glancing at her, Craig said dryly. "Someone you know?"

"My date."

"Figures."

When they reached her apartment, he pulled over to the curb and left the engine running.

"Want to talk about it now?" He reached over to remove a broken paper drink umbrella from the crown of her head.

She couldn't look at him. She felt humiliated at having gotten into the situation and even more so for having to call him to come get her. But he'd come to her rescue without question. He deserved an explanation at the very least.

"Becky talked me into going out with her cousin." Her voice was barely above a whisper. "We had dinner, he wanted to go somewhere to talk, I didn't but I went anyway, he'd had too much to drink, I lost patience with him, slipped out and called you."

Craig observed the bits of maraschino cherries and limes staining her blouse. "Where did you eat? At a Carmen Miranda convention?"

"No, Antonio's. A waitress dumped a tray of glasses on me."

"Who is this guy that subjected you to this?"

"Ricky Lawrence."

"The football player?"

"Lord. You know him, too?" She closed her eyes for a moment, too weary to think.

"Hey, mind if I get some sleep myself?" he said softly.

Temple blinked, realizing that she'd dozed off. The dashboard clock indicated it was after three in the morning. It was going to be a short night.

"I'm sorry. Thanks for coming," she said, opening the door.

"I'll walk you up."

"You don't have—"

"I'll walk you up," he repeated, getting out of the car.

They rode up in the elevator in silence. At her door, he took the key, opened the door and stepped inside, flicking on the light.

"Need anything?" he asked.

"No, thanks. I just want to take a shower and go to bed. Thanks, again."

"Hey," he said softly. "You know me. I'm the Lone Ranger, Superman and Zorro all rolled into one. Anytime you need me, I'm here." His gaze swept over her disheveled appearance again. "Just don't do something this stupid again. Okay?"

"I'm a big girl," she whispered.

"I worry about you."

"Thanks—I worry about you, too," she said as he left.

Closing the door, she leaned against it. A moment later, the doorbell rang.

Opening the door, she found Craig standing there. He handed her the broken drink umbrella, leaned over and kissed her good-night.

Looping her arms around his neck, she returned the kiss, drowning in love.

"See you in the morning," he whispered against her mouth.

She closed the door, and peeled off her clothes, leaving a trail of sticky, beer-and-fruit-stained clothing on her way to the shower.

"TEMPLE! You look fabulous!"

Temple opened the door Friday to find Nancy standing there, looking smashing. The years hadn't changed her a bit. Tanned, trim, athletic and beautiful.

"Nancy! Look at you!"

"I know you invited me to stay here with you," Nancy said, brushing past her and dropping her purse on the couch, "but I got a hotel room. I didn't know what your schedule was and I didn't want to be in your way."

"In my way? Silly! I would have loved having you here." The two women hugged.

"It's been so long!" Nancy said.

"Hasn't it?"

Greetings dispensed with, they walked arm in arm to the balcony for coffee.

"It would have been like old times, sitting up and talking half the night," Nancy allowed, "but I've got a little business to take care of and I'm not sure what my own schedule is." She sat down and kicked off her shoes. "I'm beat. Had a hard day yesterday and caught a plane early this morning. I don't know why we do it."

"Because we love it," they said in unison.

It was an old line they'd used while in flight school to help break the tension of studying.

"Well, tell me what's going on in your life," Nancy said.

"Not much, just flying and getting ready to fly." Temple poured them each a cup of coffee.

They chatted for a while, and then Nancy asked the inevitable question.

"How's Craig? Still as handsome as ever?"

"Still as handsome as ever," Temple said, feeling a twinge of guilt. Still as handsome as ever.

Suddenly, a thought hit her. Nancy always asked about Craig, but as far as she knew, they hadn't seen each other since he'd left Virginia. What would happen if she put them together again? Innocently, of course. But she could, easily.

Burney, you're treading on dangerous ground.

True, but what if I got them together? See if there's still a spark there?

The possibility that there was, hurt, but she wanted to know—no, she needed to know.

No, she amended yet again, she had to know.

"I DIDN'T KNOW The Mexican Hat was still open," Nancy marveled as they entered the small café that evening. The building was designed like a hacienda, complete with patios and porches. The interior was dimly lit by candles and wrought-iron sconces in the walls.

The structure looked about ready to fall down, but the food was outstanding. Nancy laughed. "I thought the place would be condemned by now."

"It should be, but the food's too good."

The women were led to a booth and given a huge basket of tortilla chips and salsa. Perusing the menu, Nancy grinned.

"Let's pig out," she said.

"I'm game."

"I'm going for the enchiladas," Nancy said, laying aside her menu. "Three of them, with refried beans and rice."

"Me, too," Temple said, hoping she had a good supply of antacids at home.

Sitting back in the booth, Nancy studied her. "Gee, Temple, you look great. I mean it."

"Thanks, Nance, you do, too."

"Any interesting men on the horizon?"

Smiling, Temple shook her head.

"Well, I have some new— Oh my Lord!" Nancy sat up straighter in the booth. "Is that—it is! There's Craig!"

Nancy stood up, trying to get his attention. Temple wished the ground would open up and swallow her. She had set the poor man up like a sheep going to slaughter.

"Craig! Over here!" Nancy called. "Oh, my gosh," she said under her breath. "I can't believe it. I never dreamed I'd bump into him."

Temple would've believed it. She knew Craig ate here every Friday night. She couldn't meet his eyes as he approached.

"Nancy. This is a surprise." Craig paused before the table, his eyes pinpointing Temple. "Temple."

"Fancy meeting you here," Temple murmured. Reaching for a chip, she dunked it in salsa, unaware she had targeted the hot dish. Fire broke out in her mouth, and she fumbled for her water glass.

Serves you right, ratfink. He'll never forgive you for setting him up like this—unless it works out, in which case you'll never forgive yourself.

Craig was obviously uncomfortable with the situation, but Nancy was pleased as punch to see him.

"I can't believe it! Craig! It's so good to see you," Nancy gushed. "It's been so long."

"Yes." He smiled. "What? Five years."

Temple chanced a look. She could see the tightness forming around his mouth.

"You're probably meeting someone, but sit down for a minute, will you? I've kept up with you through Temple." Nancy grinned, fawning over him.

"Have you?" Pulling out a chair, he sat down.

"Gosh, you look good," Nancy said. Her eyes reflected her admiration. "How are you?"

"Good. You?"

"Wonderful."

Squeezing his arm, she gritted her teeth, speaking affectionately, "Actually, I'm so glad we bumped into each other."

Craig's eyes moved to Temple. "Oh?"

"Yes." She leaned closer. "I wanted to apologize."

Surprise flickered in Craig's eyes. "Apologize?"

"Yes." Turning to Temple, she said. "You knew how upset I was when Craig broke off the relationship."

Craig and Temple both looked uncomfortable now. Temple hoped Nancy wouldn't make a scene. This was her second chance with Craig, possibly a new beginning, surely she wouldn't spoil it.

"What you don't know, Temple, is how ghastly I behaved."

"Nancy, it's none of my business," Temple murmured.

"Nancy," Craig warned. "It's not necessary to get into this—"

"But I want to, Craig. Really." Nancy's eyes mirrored remorse. "I've felt so bad about what happened, but I knew you wanted no further contact with me, so I quit trying to call you. I don't know why I did the stupid things I did . . . maybe because I was hurt and angry, but that's no excuse."

"Things?" Temple asked.

"Things like . . . coating his apartment with Preparation H—"

Temple's gaze flicked to Craig.

Nancy shrugged. "It seemed appropriate, considering what he'd done and how I felt." She smiled. "But that didn't ease my wounded ego, so I smashed bananas into the interior of his car . . . that helped some," she admitted.

"It was at least a hundred degrees in that car, Nancy!"

"I know that, Craig, why do you think I smashed bananas in it? Revenge isn't revenge unless it's revenge, silly."

Temple didn't know what to say, and Craig refused to look at her. She'd had no idea the breakup had been so ugly. Craig had never said a word.

"I was so damn angry at you, Craig Stevens," Nancy continued. "I, well, kept calling because I couldn't let go. I know now that you were right, of course. The relationship would have never worked, and I'm grateful you had the foresight to recognize it."

Craig's eyes met hers. "I hope you mean that, Nancy."

"I do, Craig, with all my heart. I would have told you sooner, but I didn't think you wanted to see me—under any circumstances."

"But Nancy." Temple looked puzzled. "You always ask about Craig—you're still in love with him. I can hear it in your voice each time we talk."

Nancy laughed. "You're probably right." She glanced at Craig, smiling. "You really did a number on me, Flyboy. Fool that I am, I'll always love you, in my own way, but I've moved on," she said. "My life is so full I don't have time to moon over love lost. I'm wiser now, Craig. Because you had the courage to do what you did, I finally grew up. I'm going out with a wonderful man, and we both hope it will eventually lead to marriage."

"But you keep asking about Craig in your letters," Temple said.

"Because I wanted to know that he was doing okay, silly!" Nancy turned back to Craig. "I'm happy, Craig. And a great deal of the credit goes to you. I wanted to make sure you were happy, too."

"That's wonderful," Temple managed to say, surprised by the turn of events.

"Forgive me, Craig?"

"You come near my car with bananas—"

"I won't, I promise." She laughed, crossing her heart and giving the Girl Scout sign.

Craig leaned over, and kissed Nancy lightly on the lips. When Nancy started to deepen the kiss, he pulled away, shaking his finger at her.

Grinning, she shrugged. "A girl's gotta try, hasn't she?"

Craig stood, pointing a finger at Temple. "You and I will talk later."

As he left the table, Nancy laughed with relief. "Thanks, pal."

Temple lifted her eyebrows. "For what?"

"For setting this up."

"What makes you think—"

"You never could be devious, Temple. Face it. Besides, I knew if I mentioned Craig's name, you'd make sure we bumped into each other."

Temple reached for a chip. "I feel so used."

"Don't. I needed to get that behind me, and I desperately wanted to tell him how much I appreciated what he did back then. He never told you what happened?"

"Never. Not a word." She only wished he had.

"It figures," Nancy said. "He's too much of a gentleman to air his dirty laundry in public."

But I'm not public, Temple thought. I'm Temple, his best friend. He should have told me.

"I honestly didn't know how you felt about him," Temple admitted.

"I would have told you, but I was too embarrassed. He's a great guy," Nancy said. "I often wished things could have been different between us, but they weren't and that's okay. I was a spoiled brat, and he didn't want to take on the project of raising me. He was right to break up the relationship. Better then than five years later." She picked up her menu. "Gee, spilling one's guts makes one ravenous. What shall we have for dessert that's sinfully rich and definitely not on my diet."

Still reeling from what had just transpired, Temple stared at the menu without seeing it.

Okay, Burney, your one remaining excuse for not falling for Craig is gone. Now what?

12

Setting two soft drinks in front of Craig and Scotty, Ginny laughed. "Where'd you get the shiner?"

Craig studied the purple strip turning green beneath his left eye in the mirror behind the lunch counter, frowning.

"The ex from Virginia track you down?" Scotty popped the tab on a can of soda and poured it into his glass.

"Actually, she did." For years, he'd successfully avoided Nancy. Now Temple was avoiding him. "But I got the black eye from in-line skating."

"In-line skating?" Scotty laughed.

"Celia's into in-line skating."

"Celia being the tall, well-built, athletic blonde Pete set you up with?"

"Well-built? I didn't notice—maybe because I was flat on my back the two hours we spent together."

"Wow." Ginny grinned evilly. "On your back?"

"Sprawled, Ginny," he said. "And it wasn't a pretty sight. I told her I didn't in-line skate, but she insisted anyone could in-line skate."

"I told her I couldn't skate, period, but she told me to stop being so modest. 'You look athletic, and you've got good coordination,'" he mocked in a lilting imitation of a feminine voice.

"And you proved her wrong."

"Did I ever." He touched his cheek gingerly, wincing. He recounted the incident to his friends.

Sunday had been a beautiful day, he told them, and Celia was a beautiful woman. All long tanned legs stretching a mile from short white shorts, and a great smile. The park had been full of weekend sports enthusiasts.

"Don't you just love it?" she'd enthused.

Actually, he didn't. He didn't even like it. He'd never been a park kind of guy. Baseball, football, okay. But more as a spectator than a participant. He supposed he'd spent too much time in the cockpit of a plane to enjoy strolling in the park.

But Celia was obviously an outdoors fiend. Flinging her arms wide, she drew a deep, cleansing breath, expanding her 34A to a 38C. An impressive feat.

"Wouldn't you rather take a drive?" he suggested.

"No. Come on, spoilsport. I'll bet you can use the exercise. Nothing like fresh air to make a body feel good."

Well, she was a fine example of a good body.

Celia helped him get the blades on and hauled him to his feet. He was wobbly, but she was encouraging.

"Careful—"

His feet shot out from under him, arms flailing, and he slammed head-on into a tree trunk.

Celia burst into laughter, then belatedly covered her mouth with both hands.

His ears were ringing and he shook his head to clear it, peering up at her through a fog.

"Come on, now," she said. "Concentrate, Craigee. You can do it."

Getting back on his feet, he managed to remain upright all of thirty seconds before his feet went into a frenzied scissors kick and he was down again.

"If you can walk, you can in-line-skate," Celia said.

At this point, he wasn't sure he could even walk.

Grasping his arm, she hauled him up again. By this time, they'd attracted a crowd, though people were being circumspect and watching from a distance.

"Come on," she encouraged. "Hang on to me."

Practically crawling up her leg, Craig tried to steady himself. It was a matter of pride now.

Holding on to Celia, he managed to move both feet ahead about six inches before they started leaving him. Arms frantically whipping the air, he went down again; this time taking her with him.

She laughed and together they crawled upright again. Before he knew it, he was hurtling downhill, forty, then fifty miles an hour and picking up speed. Wind stung his eyes and he wondered which was worse—blading this fast anticipating the fall, or the fall itself, for sure as hell he was going down again.

"Yes!" Celia cried out. "That's it! Now you're getting the hang of it!"

He was! And it actually felt good!

Oh, God. He was going too fast. His feet were getting ahead of him—

The next thing he knew, he'd bulldozed two mature trees with his face.

When he'd opened his eyes this time, he was strapped to a gurney in the hospital emergency room. It felt as if every bone in his body was shattered.

"Lie still, Mr. Stevens," the doctor ordered.

He groaned. "How many broken ribs?" He'd be off work for weeks.

"You were lucky. A few bruises and abrasions. That eye's going to be a shiner by morning," she told him.

"Thanks." He closed his eyes.

"I'll write you a prescription for painkillers and you can go home."

Wishing he was already home so he didn't have to move, Craig made a vow. No more wheels.

"I decided," he ended his story, "that if God wanted wheels on my feet, he'd have put them there personally."

"Tough break." Scotty chuckled.

Wiping off the counter, Ginny suddenly stopped and waved at someone behind them. "Temple's here."

"I can see that," Craig mumbled.

"She hates exercise."

Craig stared at his soda broodingly. It was now close to a week since Temple had spoken to him in anything other than monosyllables, and then only when she brought coffee to the cockpit. He knew why she was avoiding him. She thought she had violated some sacred code that night in Houston. Hell, she hadn't even acknowledged that the incident had happened. But she couldn't avoid him forever. Eventually, they'd have to talk about it.

CRAIG AND SCOTTY were going through the preflight checklist when Temple brought their coffee. She was wearing her hair in a French roll, her cap tilted pertly over her right eyebrow, and she smelled of vanilla. She looked rested, prettier than ever, or was he was just looking closer than usual?

"Hi, guys," she said cheerfully.

"Hello." Scotty reached for his flight bag. "Got a little something for you. From me and the captain."

"For me? Why?"

"Because you're so special," Scotty said.

"Gee, thanks." She laughed warily. "I didn't know you cared."

Avoiding Craig's gaze, she opened the little box Scotty handed her. It was a bar pin with the inscription O. MISS in block letters.

"What's this?"

Scotty looked puzzled. "That's your name, isn't it? O. Miss, can you bring me more coffee? O. Miss, would you dispose of my barf bag, please?' "

Temple grinned. "Why, you're right. Thank you. I shall wear this with pride."

She pinned it on her breast pocket in place of her official name tag.

Craig dropped his clipboard in a side pocket with a decided thump. "Scotty, can you find something to occupy yourself for a couple of minutes? I'd like a word with Temple."

"Talk away, I won't listen." He grinned, his eyebrows arched in an innocent look.

"In private, Scotty."

"'Scuse me. Just had a nature call."

Temple stepped aside as Scotty squeezed past her, shutting the cockpit door behind him.

She looked at Craig apprehensively. "What's going on?"

He tossed his sunglasses on the console. "That's what I want to find out."

"Craig—"

"Sit down."

"Maybe I don't want to sit—"

"Sit down, Temple."

The tight anger in his voice was very unusual. She sat.

"If it's about Nancy, I had no idea—"

"It has nothing to do with Nancy."

She sat for a moment, thinking.

"It's about us," he said. "You and me. We can't avoid each other forever."

He was right. They couldn't avoid each other forever, although she had been working at it. She wasn't ready to talk about what had happened in Houston.

When he didn't go on, she finally looked up at him.

His voice was firm, final. "Dinner. Tonight, seven o'clock. O'Kief's."

Well, whatever she'd expected, this wasn't it. She hesitated, then stood.

His gaze locked with hers. "Don't stand me up."

Not trusting her voice, she nodded, then left the cockpit.

Scotty was leaning against the bulkhead. "Everything okay?"

"Just ducky," she said. Throughout the flight, Temple was all thumbs. She delivered wrong beverages, stepped on an elderly woman's foot and dropped a full pot of coffee in the galley. The flight seemed endless.

After checking out that afternoon, she walked to her truck, stopping short when she saw Craig's Lincoln sitting perfectly between the lines of his parking space.

Tears smarted her eyes.

See. Things have changed between us. The things I loved most about our relationship. The comfortableness, the trust—the lane sharking. A sob caught in her throat. *You've done it now, Burney. It's gone. All gone.*

O'KIEF'S WAS QUIET for a weeknight. Craig and Temple followed the waiter to a booth in the corner well away from the noisy kitchen. Tension was almost palpable as they scanned the menu and placed their orders. When the waiter left, Craig released an audible breath. Resting his forearms on the table, he leaned forward and let his gaze roam over her face. Temple studied him in return. She didn't want to recognize how good he looked to her in the blue oxford shirt and navy blazer. She was having enough trouble thinking straight.

"I thought you'd at least call me," he said.

Not trusting her voice, Temple stared at her water glass.

"Okay, let's have it," he said. "What's bothering you?"

"Nothing."

"Something's wrong," he insisted. "I'm not blind. You've barely said three words to me all week that weren't work-related."

"Nonsense. It's...your imagination."

"Is it my imagination that you've stopped lane-sharking that piece of junk you drive? You've parked right for the past week."

"I haven't!" Glancing worriedly around, she lowered her voice. "You're the one who started parking right, not me."

"I'm parking right because you're parking right!"

"Craig, if I have been parking right, it's certainly been unintentional."

"I don't think so. I think it's something else."

Had she been so preoccupied lately that she'd forgotten to torment him?

He studied her for a long moment and she had the insane urge to cry.

"I...I don't know what's wrong," she said.

"I don't, either. I just know that I miss you," he said softly.

The knot in her stomach tightened. "I miss you, too," she whispered.

The silence between them held for several moments.

"Tell me about Nancy," he said.

She knew this was coming, but knowing it didn't soften the sharp feeling of jealousy and embarrassment.

"What about her?"

"What was she doing in town?"

"Taking care of business, she said."

"She said that you two have kept in touch over the years. How come I didn't know that?"

"You don't know everything," she managed to say.

"Don't you think that might have been something I wanted to know?"

With exaggerated fascination, she studied a drop of water making its way down the glass. "I...thought it would be painful for you. You never talked about her, you ended the relationship..."

He let the silence stretch for an unreasonably long time.

"You thought I still had feelings for her," he said at last.

"Yes."

"I thought we trusted each other—"

She looked up in surprise. "I do trust you!"

"Then if you ever have a question about something that affects me, like Nancy, or anything else, talk to me about it. Understand?"

"Okay." She felt incredibly foolish.

"Just to clear the record. I knew it wouldn't work between me and Nancy. Anything more you want to ask?"

"No."

"You sure? It seems there are a lot of things left unsaid between us."

"I'm sure."

Now it was his turn to find the tabletop fascinating. "I've thought a lot about what happened that night in Houston." Craig drew a deep breath. "If you want my opinion, it's been too long coming."

Temple weighed the mixture of feelings inside her. Then, as if Grams were speaking to her audibly, she heard the words: Take a chance, Tootie.

"I'm scared of what happened, Craig." She turned her water glass around, watching the rings it made on the tablecloth. "Lately...I have dreams. About you. And me."

He smiled, letting that dimple wink in his cheek. "So? I've had the same dreams."

She glanced up. "You have?"

"Temple, why does what happened between us bother you so much? Wasn't it good for you?"

Her face warmed with embarrassment. "Of course it was. It was...wonderful, but things changed that night."

"Nothing changed."

"I don't want to lose what we have," she said quietly.

His features were solemn. "Neither do I."

She straightened her silverware; smoothed the napkin, making sure the hems were even.

"Craig, let's forget that night ever happened." She made herself meet his gaze. Was there disappointment there? Or relief? "If we don't let it change things, then it won't. We can put this behind us. Forget it ever happened. Be ourselves again."

"Is that what you want?"

"It's the only way to get back to normal."

Craig sat quietly, thinking about the proposal. She drank water she didn't want.

"Craig."

"Yes."

"Even if I want things to be different, you understand it just can't be."

His gaze held hers, and she felt herself weakening.

Okay, so Nancy's out of the way, and I'm still scared.

Picking up her glass, she worked at keeping her tone light. "To us, and to normalcy," she toasted.

He hesitated, but finally touched his glass to hers. "To normalcy."

They ate dinner and carried on a nearly regular conversation. He told her about his date with Celia, and she told him about the date with Brian and they managed to laugh together.

"Temple," he said a while later, "I want your promise that you won't arrange any more dates for me. As of tonight, I'm officially off the dating circuit."

She frowned. "Are you sure?"

"I've never been more sure of anything. Tomorrow, I'm serving notice to my friends that I'll find my own dates from now on. If I have another date from hell it'll be of my own choosing."

"Yeah . . . well, I guess the same goes for me. The Ricky incident capped it off for me."

"I should hope so."

"I didn't want to go, but I let myself be persuaded. I should have paid attention to my intuition. From now on, I will."

Lifting his glass, he toasted her. "To no more blind dates."

"Hear, hear."

"I have to admit you're a big improvement over my recent dates," Craig said as he walked her to her truck later.

"Yeah. I'm glad we're back to normal."

"So am I." He leaned down and briefly touched his lips to hers.

"I'm glad we got this settled."

"So am I." Standing on tiptoe, she returned his kiss. Their lips touched once, twice, then came back together hungrily.

For a moment, the world faded as his lips explored hers. Murmuring his name incoherently, she pressed closer and closer, realizing this was hardly a friendly peck between friends.

His hands dropped to her hips and pulled her flush against him. She felt the devastating effect she was having on him. He was having the same effect on her, and she knew it had to stop now or there wouldn't be any stopping. She would drag him home to her bed like a cavewoman and he wouldn't see daylight for days.

"I have to go," she whispered, breaking away abruptly.

He drew a deep breath and released it slowly, running his fingers through his hair. "Yeah. Me, too."

As she drove away, Temple knew nothing was back to normal. It never would be again.

13

THE SILVERADO SAT in its usual place every day the next week. Squarely on the line between the two parking places. Craig had to squeeze the Lincoln into his spot as best he could. At least that much was normal.

On Thursday, when they still hadn't had their usual race for the space, he squeezed out of his car. As he passed Temple's truck, he laid a hand on the hood. Cool. She'd been in for at least an hour. The truce they'd agreed to hadn't made any difference. She was still avoiding him.

Giving Flo the high sign as he passed the car rental booth, Craig strode quickly to the staff lounge. Scotty was already there, a cup of coffee, a checkbook and a pile of envelopes in front of him. Pouring himself some coffee, Craig observed dryly in his best "Twilight Zone" imitation, "For your consideration, Jim Scott, pilot. Checkbook. Pile of envelopes. Frown. It is . . . the first of the month."

"Forget the 'Twilight Zone.' This is more a David Copperfield thing," Scotty retorted. "The trick is seeing how far the ole paycheck will stretch. This month, I don't think it's going to stretch far enough."

Craig took a chair across from his copilot. "A wife, three kids, a mortgage, car payments. How do you do it?"

Scotty closed the checkbook and stuffed the envelopes into his jacket pocket. "It's not easy, but Steph and I think she needs to be home with the kids right now."

Looking away, Craig's features clouded.

"Something bothering you?" Scotty asked.

"Not really." He took a sip of his coffee.

"Temple?"

Shrugging, Craig stared at the cup as if analyzing it. "Want to talk about it?"

"No, not yet."

Scotty briefly rested a hand on Craig's shoulder as he got up. "You know where I am. Shoulder's free."

Scotty went to mail his monthly payments. Craig was staring at his cooling coffee and brooding when Temple walked in a few moments later.

"Hi," she said.

"Hi."

"Any plans for tonight?"

Surprised, he glanced up. "Tentative. You?"

"I'm filling in for Janeanne on a Chicago flight. Did Susan call you?"

The muscle in Craig's jaw tightened. "No more dates, Temple. That's gospel."

"I know we agreed, but I'm in a bind," she told him. "Susan cornered me yesterday. We'd talked some time ago about, well, setting up something with you. She kind of pinned me down for tonight."

"No."

Temple poured a half cup of coffee and sipped it hesitantly. "Is that a flat no, or a semi-flat no?"

Hell. What's the use, he thought. Obviously she wasn't really ready to let this thing between them, whatever it was, develop into anything.

"What's she look like?"

The question obviously took Temple by surprise. Apparently, she was expecting him to hold out, plead burnout, tell her to lay off.

That's the problem, he thought. We've always had this "best buddy" thing working, use each other for an excuse to get out of a date or to come to the rescue—like the Ricky Lawrence incident—and now she's taking me for granted. I'm always around when she needs me. I'm too available. As for the other night, who the hell knew what she was thinking.

Glancing at his watch, he stood. "It's getting late."

"What do I tell Susan?"

He reached for his sunglasses and slid them on. "Tell her to wear a red dress if she has one."

SUSAN WAS A KNOCKOUT. Tall, blond, sense of humor and legs that wouldn't quit.

Craig had to admit she tried hard to please. He couldn't seem to make the effort at small talk so she'd carried most of the conversation during dinner.

He tried to concentrate on what she was saying, but failed. His thoughts were on Temple. Her flight to Chicago was predicted to hit some heavy snow in the Midwest. She was flying in an ATR twin-engine turboprop. The French-made commuter had been experiencing problems with icing recently. A debate was ongoing whether or not to ground the plane during inclement weather.

Why worry, Stevens? She'll be down by midnight, the storm isn't due until closer to morning. The pilot's experienced. Since when did flying cause you reason for alarm?

"Dinner was wonderful. Is this a favorite place of yours?"

Craig pulled his thoughts back to Susan. She was beautiful, intelligent, worked for two of the city's prominent attorneys. The evening was turning out to be pleasant, so why was he finding it so hard to concentrate?

"The Bird's Nest? Actually, Temple found this restaurant. She's partial to their prime rib."

Susan leaned forward, smiling, her inquisitive green eyes meeting his. "You've known Temple a long time?"

"A long time." His gaze returned to the window to study the bank of low clouds moving in.

Stop worrying about her, Stevens. She's okay.

A couple of hours later, he paid the bar tab while Susan went to the rest room. The evening had gone smoothly. The first date in a month that hadn't been a disaster. The news should make Temple happy.

Susan had come in a cab so he'd offered to take her home. Afterward, he'd go work out at the gym.

When the valet brought the Lincoln around, Susan let out a squeal. "Ohhhh, a Lincoln!"

Startled, Craig turned to look at her and missed the door handle. They had just spent four-plus pleasant hours together. She hadn't giggled, snickered, prattled or yakked once.

But now she'd squealed. He'd heard it.

"Oh, I love it!" She ran a hand over the smooth finish on the fender. "May I drive it?"

The request caught him off guard. "Well—"

"Oh, thank you! I adore these big luxury cars. They're so cool to drive. Know what I mean?"

He didn't. Didn't have a clue, actually, but he acquiesced and climbed into the passenger's seat and buckled his seat belt.

As they pulled away from the curb, Susan deftly merged with the traffic and he relaxed. She seemed to know what she was doing. Maybe she just had a fetish for big cars.

She moved smoothly with the traffic flow, eventually drifting into the fast lane. The speedometer needle was on fifty when she suddenly drifted across the center line, heading straight for an oncoming car.

He lunged for the wheel, cursing. The car lurched sharply. Righting himself, he looked over at her. "What are you doing?"

The RPM needle shot upward as she looked back at him.

When she didn't say anything, he grabbed her arm to get her attention and emphasize his words. "What are you doing? Keep your eyes on the road!" he yelled over the engine's roar.

Shrugging, she appeared to concentrate, and he sat back in the seat again, eyeing her sourly.

"Sorry."

"No problem," he murmured. Mistakes happen. He thought of the synonym he could have used and deemed it more appropriate.

They had gone another five miles when she did it again. Quick reflexes were all that saved them from having a head-on with a semi.

The engine roared like a jet as they barreled down the highway, still straddling the center line.

"What are you doing?" he yelled.

She glanced at him idly. "What?"

"You're going to kill us both. Get in your lane!" He gestured to an emergency-stop area. "Pull over!" He'd had enough!

Calmly drifting back into her lane, she maneuvered through the traffic toward the ramp.

When the car stopped, he looked at her, shaken. "Why did you do that?"

"I don't know." she shrugged. "I guess I wasn't thinking."

"Drifting into the opposite lane—that's suicidal."

She seemed nonplussed. "Sorry."

"Do you want me to drive?"

"No," she said, looking offended. "I can drive."

"All right. But keep your mind on the road."

Flipping down the visor to reveal a lighted mirror, she checked her lipstick. "Will you want to have sex?"

His mouth fell open and his mind went blank.

She glanced at him, still smoothing her lipstick. "Well?"

"Um, I hadn't thought about it." He did now, and he didn't want it. Not with her.

"I'm agreeable."

He glanced behind them and indicated for her to pull back into the traffic. "Keep driving."

"I'm into handcuffs and chains," she said.

"What?"

She flipped the visor back into place, checked the traffic, then drove onto the freeway. "Do you have any fetishes? Feet do anything for you?"

He began searching for the nearest exit.

"Pull off here."

She whipped off the freeway and he managed to brace himself enough to avoid whiplash. They were approaching a traffic signal when he felt the car surge.

"The light's turning red!" he shouted.

"I can beat it." She gunned through the intersection. As they passed beneath the signal, his entire life flashed before his eyes.

"Stop!"

She slammed on the brakes, which nearly propelled him through the windshield again. Ashen-faced, he gripped the dash with white knuckles. Sweat trickled down his temples. The fish he ate for dinner soured in his stomach.

He drew a deep breath, and struggled to control his voice. "What are you doing?"

She looked at him innocently. "You said 'pull off here.'"

He leaned back, wiping sweat off his brow.

"Do you wear glasses?"

"Yes, but not when I drive," she said crossly. She pulled back onto the road. "You should have said you're nervous in traffic. I would have slowed down. Here. Is this slow enough for you?"

By the time they reached her apartment building, she had slowed to the point that cars were honking and flashing lights as they swerved around them.

Driving two miles an hour, she carefully turned the car into the driveway of her apartment building. Spotting an empty parking space, she flipped on the blinker.

The blinker. Now she puts on the blinker, he thought crossly.

Susan stopped the car, judiciously eyeing the parking space.

Finally maneuvering the big car into the space, she failed to straighten the wheels.

Instead of turning off the engine, she rummaged through her purse, fishing out her keys.

She checked her makeup in the visor mirror again. His hands clenched into fists.

Reaching into the back seat for her coat, she rummaged in a pocket.

His nerves were raw.

"The... blinker... is... on," he said, emphasizing each word.

"Hmm?"

He gritted his teeth. "You forgot to turn off the blinker."

"Okay." She flipped off the lights.

"The lights go off automatically."

"Okay." She flipped them back on. "So—want to come up?"

"I don't think so."

"You sure?"

He was positive.

Unlocking his apartment door a half hour later, he tossed his keys onto the coffee table and noticed the message light on his answering machine blinking.

Pushing the play button, he listened to Scotty's message, a knot forming in the pit of his stomach.

"If you're there, Craig, pick up." A momentary silence. "Look, uh, Temple's in trouble. You knew she took Jane-anne's flight to Chicago. There's bad weather. It came in earlier than expected and they've run into trouble. Knew you'd want to know. I'm at the tower keeping an eye on things. Hope this is over by the time you get home, buddy."

Craig turned on his heel, and headed back out the door, scooping up his keys on the way. Ten minutes later, he was speeding toward the airport.

Scotty met him at the door of the tower. Behind him Craig could see three men huddled around a table. A fourth was on the phone.

"What's going on?"

Scotty's voice was tight with tension. "Temple's ATR is hanging over Chicago. Heavy air traffic has put them in a holding pattern. There are a dozen planes they're trying to get down while they still can. The plane is experiencing heavy icing—"

Stepping into the tower, Craig joined the men gathered around the console. He could hear a voice coming over the speakerphone. Outside the glass tower the clear cool night mocked him.

One of the senior officers turned. "Stevens. What are you doing here?"

Pilots weren't supposed to be in the tower, but this, he knew, would be an exception. It didn't hurt that Craig was considered a top-notch pilot and might be able to lend some experience to the situation.

"Are you in contact with the plane?" he asked.

"Yeah," the man said. "We've got Temple on the phone."

Craig leaned over the speaker.

"Temple?"

"Craig? Oh, I'm so glad you're there."

Craig sat down, blocking out his surroundings. All that he was conscious of was the fear in Temple's voice.

"What's going on, sweetheart?"

"It's not good."

"How are you doing?"

"About...about as well as a turkey the day before Thanksgiving."

He smiled slightly, reading the attempt to keep him from hearing the stress in her voice.

"We're monitoring things here," he told her. "Who's the pilot?"

"Dave DeCosta."

"How many on board, Temple?"

"Sixty-four passengers, four crew."

Her voice sounded small, unsure. Frightened. He'd never heard that in her before.

"You're in good hands," he said reassuringly. "Dave knows his way around a plane." Craig glanced up at the strained faces circling him. "Are you really all right?"

"A little nervous, uh, we're in a holding pattern at...eight thousand feet."

The air controller closest to Craig leaned in and spoke directly into his ear so Temple wouldn't hear. "Wind gusts to fifty miles per hour, ground temperature thirty-two degrees and falling. Rain turning to freezing rain, blowing almost horizontally. If he'd been a half hour earlier, they'd have made it easy. The front moved in faster than the tower anticipated, hanging up several flights. Air-traffic control in Chicago is trying to get them down in order. The ATR's last in line."

A list of the recent spate of accidents involving the commuter during bad weather flashed through Craig's mind. Perfectly safe, except in extreme conditions. And these conditions were extreme.

"What's O'Hare saying?"

"They've got their hands full," the official said. "It's a real bitch. An inch of ice and more falling. The crew's trying to clear a couple of runways, but they're not making much headway. The runways ice over almost as fast as they can clear. They need a break real bad."

"Craig?"

The quaver in Temple's voice told Craig how scared she was. The others glanced at one another, indicating they'd heard it, too. The chief ran a hand down his face in frustration and concern.

"I'm here," Craig told her.

"I'm glad. But you always have been," she said, her voice higher and lighter than normal. "I guess... I guess I've abused that, in a way. I'm sorry. About everything. I just... I just didn't want to lose— Can you forgive me?"

"Temple, honey... we'll talk later."

"Craig?"

"Yeah." He hated hearing the fear in her voice, hated not being able to talk to her alone, to tell her everything would be all right and make her believe it.

"If... if we don't get a chance to talk—"

"Temple, get hold of yourself—"

Her words came in a rush. "But if we don't, I have to say this. I've been doing a lot of thinking. About... about us.

About what happened . . . that night. I'm glad it happened. I might never have known— I've been an idiot, Craig. Up here, well, I can see everything clearly now."

"Temple—" He turned his back to the others and lowered his voice. In a calm voice, he said, "This isn't the way it's supposed to be. There should be candles, low lights, wine, you in my arms, not you in some damned machine eight thousand feet aboveground and me here. When you get down, we'll talk about this—"

Temple didn't seem to hear him. "I talked to Grams about us. I told her I was worried. She's a smart lady. She told me that things now aren't so different than when she was young. She made me realize that what I . . . what I feel for you isn't wrong. It's right. Very right. I just wasn't sure what it was. And I wasn't sure how you felt—I know we agreed not to talk about it—"

Suddenly reminded that they were on a speakerphone, Craig looked up into the face of one of the women air-traffic controllers. Accusation was clear in her dark eyes. She obviously thought he was the biggest jerk of all time. He wasn't sure he disagreed.

The men were studying him with speculation.

"Temple—"

"No, don't stop me. I want to say this. I've got to say it, in case— I want you to know . . . I've known for weeks. I just couldn't admit it to myself. You know, the antipilot-relationship thing, and Nancy. Well, I know they were just excuses because I was scared. But I . . . I can't leave without saying it—"

"You're not 'leaving.' Where's your training?"

"Training? I forgot every word of it about thirty minutes ago."

He closed his eyes, aching to hold her. Aching to tell her he felt the same.

"I love you, Craig. I have for a long time—" Her voice broke and his hands clenched. "I was just too . . . blind to recognize it."

"Temple—"

A sniff drew his attention to the group crowding close. The air-traffic controller who'd glared at him so accusingly now had tears in her eyes. She stood with one hand covering her mouth.

Scotty stood nearby, listening soberly, his gaze locking with Craig's when he looked up.

"Don't stop me," Temple continued. "I want you to know that I love you. And that night in Houston? I wasn't asleep. I knew you were making love to me. I deliberately led you on...because I had to know—"

"I've fallen in love with you, and it scares me," she said in a rush of words. "We were so close and I was so afraid things would change. I...I didn't—" A sob broke her voice. "I didn't want to lose what we had by taking a chance on more. And it has changed things, hasn't it? It's changed everything. Nothing's been the same between us since—"

"Temple, we'll talk about this later—"

"No! I don't have any more time to waste. I've wasted too much already. I knew your every thought, the things you like, the things you don't like. We could always talk about anything. I guess that's what makes our relationship so special. So special I didn't want to lose it." She managed a little laugh. "Well, we know each other a lot better now, don't we? I just...I just wanted to know what...what being in love was like. And now I know. At least, I know what it's like to fall in love with you." She was quiet for a moment. "It's beautiful," she whispered. "The most perfect thing anyone could ever experience. It's like...being reborn. Everything looks different, tastes different. I...I always looked forward to seeing you every day. But now...now it's as if I can't breathe until I see you..."

She let the words drift away.

"Temple?" Craig sat up straighter. "What is it?"

He glanced up at the controllers. One was on the phone and caught his gaze and held it.

"They're going to try it," the controller said softly. "The other planes are down. One skidded off the runway and there are some injuries but it looks like everything is okay.

The plows are out clearing a second runway. They're going to try putting Dave down on it. It's the only chance they've got."

"How's the wind?"

"Velocity down a bit, rain has abated a little."

Not much of a change, but it was all they had.

"Oh. Okay." Her voice came back to him over the line. "Craig, Dave's been cleared to land."

"Temple—"

Drawing a deep breath, she whispered, "I have to hang up now. Goodbye—I love you."

Then the connection was broken.

Craig sank into a chair, staring at the speakerphone, his eyes stinging.

Dammit! He hadn't told her he loved her.

14

"LADIES AND GENTLEMEN, the captain has been cleared to land. Please check your seat belts and assume the crash position. Place pillows in your lap, lean forward so your head is between your knees, lock your hands behind your head..." And pray, Temple added silently.

Temple glanced at Sarah, the other flight attendant. Her fear was mirrored in Sarah's eyes.

"You will feel a bump when we set down on the runway," she told the passengers. "Please remain in your seats until the aircraft stops moving. Every precaution has been taken for a safe landing. When I give the word, please move quickly toward exits. Parents, keep children close in front of you and hold on to them at all times. Chutes will be deployed for exits. Sarah and I will assist you onto the slide, and emergency personnel will be waiting to catch you at the bottom. Are there any questions?"

The only sound in the cabin was the engines laboring and a child whimpering.

Temple had been flying for years and this was her first emergency. She knew pilots who'd flown all their lives and never encountered trouble.

She had known some who hadn't survived.

When Dave had summoned her to the cockpit, she'd thought he wanted coffee. She'd hardly been able to comprehend the conditions he'd outlined in a tense voice. The weather had changed so swiftly everyone had been caught by surprise. Any doubts she might have had about the seriousness of the situation had been erased by the sight of the tension in the pilot's face.

Temple opened the cockpit door. "Dave, we're ready back here."

Dave nodded. "It's going to get rough."

She nodded.

Closing the door, she buckled herself into her seat, giving the passenger in 1-A a reassuring smile.

I love you, Craig. I wish we'd had more time...

Leaning forward, Temple put her head between her knees and linked her hands behind her head... and prayed.

Her ears roared as they descended and she tried not to think of the ice on the plane, nor the condition of the runway.

The plane hit the runway hard, bounced twice, the engine reversed and she heard the flaps shift. One more bounce and the plane skidded. They were going sideways down the runway; the plane turned and kept going with the brakes screaming. The skid seemed to go on forever. There was a bump, a lurch, another skid and then stillness.

A deathly silence filled the small cabin. Temple's head pounded as she clamped her eyes closed. She could hear her own heartbeat.

She waited a count of five, then unbuckled her seat belt and jumped up.

"Push those doors open!" she shouted to the men assigned to the exit doors. "Unbuckle, up-up-up!"

Women with small children were first out the doors and sliding down the escape chutes. Icy rain was falling, coating everything it touched. The red and blue lights of emergency vehicles and airport personnel flashed across the tarmac and the crackle of radios in the background mingled with shouts of frenzied directions.

As soon as passengers reached the end of the chute, someone pulled them to their feet and ushered them toward a warm airport van.

The last passenger hit the chute. Temple pushed Sarah in front of her, then followed.

Someone grabbed her arm as she hit the tarmac, and ushered her toward a waiting van. Pilot and copilot joined her and Sarah a moment later.

Grasping Dave DeCosta's hand, Temple whispered, "Thank you—every passenger aboard that plane owes you his life."

Dave squeezed her hand reassuringly, his face still showing the strain of the past twenty minutes.

As the van drove toward the terminal, Temple turned to look back at the plane.

The ATR was coated in ice. Instead of sitting on the landing wheels, it lay flat on the runway, skewed sideways and tilted like a broken toy.

"That was too close for comfort," Dave admitted, following her gaze.

They were taken to a room inside the terminal where coffee, hot chocolate, tea and food were waiting. Phones were available so passengers could call family members while luggage was unloaded and the plane secured.

Hours later, the crew finished being debriefed. Temple was called to the phone twice, first to assure Craig she was down safely, and second, to convince Craig she really was down safely.

It was past midnight when an airport shuttle delivered Temple to a hotel. Too weary to shower, and with no clean clothes to change into anyway, she stripped off her uniform and crawled into bed. The moment her head hit the pillow, she fell asleep. Only her wake-up call the next morning jarred her from slumber.

"Good morning. Any aftereffects?" Dave asked when he called to check on her.

"None, how about you?"

"Fine shape. Our flight back to Dallas leaves in an hour."

They got on the plane as passengers this time. Temple sat looking out the window as this morning's travelers boarded. The sun was shining, and while buildings were still ice-encrusted, the melting was already under way. The runways were clear, with little spirals of steam rising upward as the sun reflected off the concrete. How strange it all seemed. Last night had been so frightening, proving how quickly everything could change.

The storm—one that could not have been anticipated—had changed her life. At least she still had a life. This morning, Sparrow had announced all ATRs were grounded during inclement weather until further notice.

Dave DeCosta was due a commendation for getting the plane down without injury. There had been some bumps and scrapes as passengers exited the chutes, but nothing serious.

Temple's stomach tied in a painful knot as the plane left the ground. The butterflies calmed down as the aircraft leveled out.

In a short while, she would be back in Dallas. On one hand she could hardly wait to get there, on the other, there was Craig to face. And the tower personnel who'd listened to her blubbering over the speakerphone. Spilling every little secret, every titillating detail.

What had she been thinking? How would she ever face Craig? She'd made such a fool of herself. Blurting out everything that had happened that night in Houston. Events she'd been trying to come to terms with for weeks. What was she going to do with them now that she'd told the world her innermost secrets.

So, her personal life was in a shambles, the pieces of it laid out for everyone to see—friends, co-workers, Craig.

Not only that, but her professional life was a shambles, too. She'd never been in a close call before. Her confidence was badly shaken. She'd known that accidents were always a possibility, but accidents happened to others, not to her. Was she capable of continuing her job?

Troubled thoughts occupied her mind during the flight. She was aware of their descent into Dallas only when the flight attendant picked up the microphone—

"Ladies and gentlemen, thank you for flying Sparrow Airlines. Please replace your tables and return your seat backs to their full upright and least comfortable position—''

Ten minutes. Ten minutes and you'll walk into a terminal where everyone will know that you're in love with Craig. No more pretending he's just a friend. Just a friend. How phony that sounded. No wonder Ginny and Flo never believed you when you insisted that's all there was. It was clear to them how you felt.

She waited to be the last person off the plane, hoping to get into the terminal before anyone saw her. But it wasn't to be.

''Temple! Temple!'' Ginny was jumping up and down, waving to her from the front of a crowd of airport personnel awaiting the arrival of the stressed crew.

Hesitating, Temple wrestled with the idea of running, of taking off in the opposite direction as hard as she could walk.

Instead, she calmly walked toward Ginny, smiling. When the usually caustic waitress grabbed her and hugged her around the neck tightly, she closed her eyes against tears and hugged her back.

''We were so scared,'' Ginny said.

''Not half as scared as me,'' Temple said, trying to laugh.

Her gaze swept over the crowd. Craig was conspicuously absent. She'd spilled her guts, and clearly he hadn't wanted to hear it.

''We waited here last night until Chicago told us you were down and okay,'' Ginny told her. ''I was awake all night. I wanted to call, but I knew you'd be too busy to talk.''

''I was. Now I'm drained. I feel like I could sleep for a week.''

Others reached out to touch her, squeeze her arm, take her hand, call out her name. She was surprised and gratified by their warm reception. These really were such great people.

Her co-workers eventually dispersed, returning to their posts, and she continued through the terminal alone. Ginny waved to her again from behind the lunch counter and Flo gave her a high sign from the car rental booth. Her hand was on the handle of the glass doors leading to the parking lot before she saw him.

Craig was leaning against his car, dressed in faded and worn jeans that fit him like a glove, and a pale blue shirt. Collar open, sleeves causally rolled up, he reminded Temple of a nineties cover model. She'd never seen him look so good.

He waited, his gaze challenging her. Finally, she pushed through the doorway.

"Hi."

"Hi."

She stood, bag in hand, wondering what to say. He had called twice to see how she was last night. Why hadn't he called three times?

"Yes."

She glanced up. "Yes?"

"Yes, I feel the same way about you."

"Oh." She felt her cheeks grow warm. "Craig . . . about last night—"

"Get in," he said, motioning to the passenger side of the Lincoln.

"My truck—"

"I said, get in."

She slid into the car and waited for him to walk around to the driver's side, get in and pull out of the parking lot. Holding her breath, she was surprised when he didn't say anything.

Resting her head against the back of the seat, she looked out the window, watching passing street signs as he drove toward her apartment.

"I had to bail out once," he said, breaking the silence. "At the time, it was such a rush of adrenaline I couldn't unwind for days. When I was back on the ground, I slept— for two days."

She smiled softly. Yeah, he'd know how she felt. But then, he always did.

Temple couldn't look at him. It was coming now. How foolish she'd been, how indiscreet.

"You scared me, you know."

"I scared myself. I don't know if—if I can go back, Craig."

His gaze remained on the highway, his hands moving easily on the steering wheel. "I've been offered a job down in the Keys flying private charters."

"Oh?" Her heart raced. Had she scared him off with her public admission? Fool! You knew better! Now look what you've done!

She made her tone sound casual. "Thinking about taking it?"

"It's damn good money...yeah, I think I am considering it."

Mortified with herself, she felt tears spring to her eyes. The last thing she wanted was to make him feel guilty about leaving. Why shouldn't he take the job? More money, Florida. Sunshine, balmy breezes, beautiful women in string bikinis....

She turned her face to the window, trying to stem the tide of tears suddenly rolling down her cheeks.

Reaching over, he pulled her next to him, leaving his arm around her shoulders.

"That's better," he said.

She sighed, and rested her head against his shoulder, her hand lying on his chest, feeling his heartbeat. This felt so good, so natural. How would she live without him? Florida wasn't the end of the earth, but they both had their jobs, responsibilities that would keep them apart.

"Craig, I'm sorry about last night. I should have realized I was making a fool of myself, but I thought I was going to die without having ever told you—"

His kiss interrupted her apology. The car swerved into the center lane, and he brought it quickly back into line. Thoughts of Susan haunted him.

"Let's discuss this when we get you home."

"I need to talk to Grams," she managed to say, her head spinning.

She spent the rest of the ride napping on Craig's shoulder.

Craig pulled the Lincoln into her parking space. As he got out, he waved to Roberta King, who was down on her knees, pruning rosebushes.

Coming around to the passenger side of the car, he opened the door for Temple. "Come on, sleepyhead. You can make me breakfast."

Now it's coming, she thought. He'll wait until we're in my apartment, and then he'll let me have it. The kiss was just to keep her from making a bigger fool of herself. He'd insist they were right to remain friends. He'd go to the Keys, she'd stay in Dallas. She didn't know if she could do that.

Her apartment was the only thing that hadn't changed in the last twenty-four hours. It felt good to be home.

Dropping her flight bag on the floor, she kicked off her pumps. "I need a shower."

"Make it snappy. I'll put on coffee, and scramble eggs. Got any bacon?"

Temple disappeared into the bedroom, and Craig put bacon on to fry. Flipping on the television, he settled down to wait. The shower was still running when the bacon was done. He'd scrambled eggs and made toast, and located the strawberry jam when he heard the water finally stop.

A few minutes later, she came out of the bedroom dressed in a white terry-cloth robe, her damp hair brushed back from her face.

"Breakfast smells good."

She took blue crockery mugs out of the cabinet, wishing he'd get it over with—say something—anything!

When Craig's arms came around her from behind, she started, sending a mug clattering against the cabinet.

"A little jumpy this morning, aren't you, Burney?" His mouth brushed the nape of her neck as he loosened the sash on her robe. She forgot all about coffee.

"All right, let me have it," she whispered.

He kissed lightly down her neck, lingering at her ear. His voice was soft against her lobe. "Oh, I plan to, just as soon as we talk."

So, she was right. He was angry at her for embarrassing him.

"I'm mad as hell at you," he said, punctuating his words with kisses against her nape.

"I know—I shouldn't have—I didn't realize the whole tower was listening—" He'd never held her quite this way before. Close. Intimate. His hands spread across her midriff, molding her body into his. She could smell his cologne.

"Will you let me finish?"

"Sorry."

"Last night you hung up on me before I could answer you."

"Did I ask a question?" Parts of last night's events were a blur.

"No, but you were carrying on a conversation with me that I wasn't participating in."

"Okay." She bent her head, allowing him better access to her neck. "I'm listening. What do you want to say?"

His right hand slipped beneath the robe and captured her breast. "That I love you, too.

The near crash must have affected her hearing. "I—"

"Love you—you and me." Her heart jumped.

He turned her around to face him. "You and me. Friends and lovers. Man and wife. Mom and Dad. Grandpa and Grandma."

"Craig, I—"

He kissed her thoroughly this time, his mouth insistent, demanding on hers. As their lips parted, he whispered against them, "Nuts to this dating stuff. Will you marry me?"

"Yes." She didn't have to think about the answer. She'd thought of nothing else lately.

Their mouths merged hungrily. "No arguments about being 'just friends'?"

"None," she whispered as his hands grew more aggressive.

"No? Nothing wrong with marrying your best friend?" he murmured. "Even if he is a pilot?"

She shook her head, speechless for once in her life. She couldn't think of anything nicer.

"No more looking for Mr. Right. No more dates from hell."

"Most definitely not."

"It's about time," he breathed.

Long minutes passed before their lips parted again.

"Burney," he chided, his fingers gently slipping off the robe and letting it drop to the floor. He stepped back to look at her.

"Not fair," she said softly.

"What's not fair?"

"You're still dressed."

He grinned, and she smiled back at him, loving that dimple that winked in his cheek. He began to unbutton his shirt.

"So, you put me through that night in Houston to tease me."

"I didn't tease you." Her eyes reminded him of that night.

"No." His eyes traveled over her leisurely. "I came away satisfied."

She smiled. "Want to hear something worse?"

"What?"

"I wasn't all that cold, either."

"Want to hear something worse than that?"

She frowned, made suspicious by the look in his eyes. "What?"

"I turned off the thermostat before I got into bed."

"You didn't!"

"I did."

The eggs and bacon were long forgotten now.

"I'm glad."

"Oh, really?"

"Really," she whispered, drawing him to her now. They kissed again, his hands shockingly bold now.

"You don't happen to be into whips and chains, do you?"

She laughed. "What?"

"Foot fetishes?"

Sweeping her up into his arms, he carried her toward the bedroom.

Whips and chains? Foot what? What was he talking about? On the other hand, what did she care?

She didn't, she decided, as his mouth hungrily sought hers.

Not in the least.

Epilogue

Dear Grams,

Set two extra plates at the table this weekend. We're flying to Dallas Saturday morning. We'll come directly from the airport to your house.

Can't wait to see you, Grams! Craig and I have a surprise we think you'll like.

Love,
Tootie

"Temple?"

"In the den, darling." Temple sealed the envelope, patted her tummy and sighed contentedly. "I'm writing Grams."

"Damn grubworms are taking over the lawn." Craig came into the room, leaning down to kiss his wife. He patted her stomach. "Want to head out for ice cream? Double double chocolate cherry blitz?"

"With whip cream and butterfinger shavings?"

"Sure, why not?" Pulling her to her feet, Craig kissed his wife, lingering momentarily. His hand caressed her stomach again, giving his child a gentle squeeze. "How's Junior this morning?" he whispered.

"Junior's doing very well, thank you." Junior was little more than a speck on the ultrasound screen, but the doctor assured her he'd grow.

They stood for a moment, rocking with each other, kissing, loving each other.

"Junior could be a girl, you know," Temple said.

"I know, and if she is, I hope she's as pretty as her mother."

When their finally lips parted, he smiled. "Why don't you just call Grams and tell her about the baby?"

"No way. I want to see the look on her face when I tell her she's finally going to be a great-grandmother!"

Giving her one last kiss on the tip of her nose, he moseyed in to the kitchen for a cold drink. "Did you tell her we're planning to spend a week with her?"

"Yes, and she'll be so excited. Since we've moved to the Keys, I don't see her nearly as often as I'd like."

"Well, if everything goes as planned, she can help us celebrate. It isn't every day we buy our own charter company."

Temple decided she and Craig would do some of their own private celebrating after their guests went home. "Oh, Craig, I hope Thia likes Keith. They would make a perfect couple!"

"Better tread lightly, Temple. Keith gets skittish when anyone mentions the word *marriage.*

"I know, so does Thia, but they seemed so right for each other."

"Yeah." Draping his arm around her neck, he walked her toward the garage door. "Listen, there's this new pilot at work? Neil Petersen? He just moved down here, and he seems kind of lonesome. I'm always talking about you and the baby, and I see him get this faraway look in his eye. Do you think Sue would be interested—"

"Sue? Well, she hates for us to 'set her up,' as she calls it, but sure, I can arrange a small dinner party when we get back from visiting Grams. I'll call her and see when she plans to be in town," Temple said. "She's back flying commuters again. She got tired of the international flights. Week after next be soon enough?"

"That'll be fine."

"I'll fix pork chops."

"You're a doll." He pulled her to him for another quick kiss.

"Listen to us, we sound like Scotty and Steph!" Temple exclaimed.

"Scotty and Steph!" Craig laughed. "No way!"

"Yeah, you're right. This is different. Sue is such a good friend, it's a shame she hasn't found Mr. Right yet. We're not being matchmakers, we're just being concerned friends."

"Right."

"Absolutely, right."

Opening the door to the garage, Craig helped her down the small flight of steps. The new, four-door Jimmy sat where the Lincoln used to.

"Okay, so, I'll casually invite Neil to drop by, and you have Sue here . . ."

Harlequin® Historical

If you're a serious fan of historical romance,
then you're in luck!

Harlequin Historicals brings you
stories by bestselling authors, rising new stars
and talented first-timers.

Ruth Langan & Theresa Michaels
Mary McBride & Cheryl St.John
Margaret Moore & Merline Lovelace
Julie Tetel & Nina Beaumont
Susan Amarillas & Ana Seymour
Deborah Simmons & Linda Castle
Cassandra Austin & Emily French
Miranda Jarrett & Suzanne Barclay
DeLoras Scott & Laurie Grant...

You'll never run out of favorites.

Harlequin Historicals...they're too good to miss!

HH-GEN

HARLEQUIN  PRESENTS®

HARLEQUIN PRESENTS
men you won't be able to resist falling in love with...

HARLEQUIN PRESENTS
women who have feelings just like your own...

HARLEQUIN PRESENTS
powerful passion in exotic international settings...

HARLEQUIN PRESENTS
intense, dramatic stories that will keep you turning
to the very last page...

HARLEQUIN PRESENTS
The world's bestselling romance series!

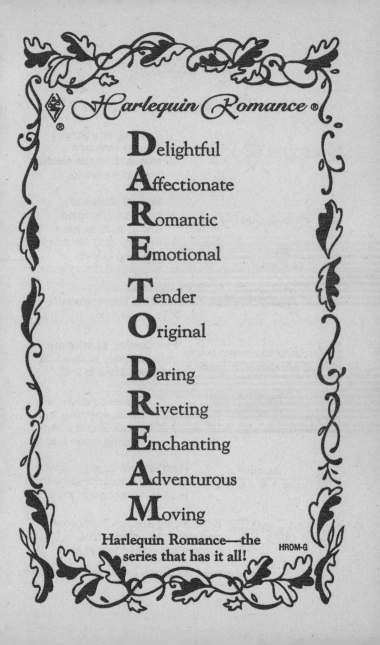

Harlequin Romance ®

Delightful

Affectionate

Romantic

Emotional

Tender

Original

Daring

Riveting

Enchanting

Adventurous

Moving

Harlequin Romance—the
series that has it all!

HROM-G

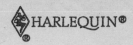 **HARLEQUIN®**

Not The Same Old Story!

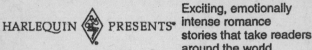

Exciting, emotionally intense romance stories that take readers around the world.

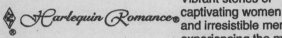

Vibrant stories of captivating women and irresistible men experiencing the magic of falling in love!

Bold and adventurous—Temptation is strong women, bad boys, great sex!

Provocative, passionate, contemporary stories that celebrate life and love.

Romantic adventure where anything is possible and where dreams come true.

Heart-stopping, suspenseful adventures that combine the best of romance and mystery.

LOVE & LAUGHTER™ Entertaining and fun, humorous and romantic—stories that capture the lighter side of love.